"Did you find a date for the wedding?"

She blinked, stunned by the change of topic.

"I'll go," he said. "You stay here for the time you promised and I'll go with you to your sister's wedding."

As much as she hated to admit it, his offer was really, really tempting. Even so, she found herself answering, "I couldn't ask you to do that."

"Too bad. You already did, Friday night. Now I'm accepting."

She considered leaving via that closed door and refusing Gage's offer. Her pride told her to bolt and never look back. There was only one problem. She needed him.

Almost as much as he needed her.

* * *

Temporary to Tempted
is part of the Bachelor Pact series
from Jessica Lemmon.

Dear Reader,

What happens when the person you hire sight unseen ends up being the same woman who approached you in a bar recently and offered to *pay you* to go with her to a wedding?

Andy Payne is single...and desperate. She can't bear the idea of showing up to her youngest sister's destination wedding alone. When the hot guy at the bar shoots down her offer, Andy never expects to see him again, but come Monday, Andy learns Gage is her client!

After a brief negotiation, they end up flying across the country to attend the wedding together. As the lines between pretend and real start to blur, Andy's ice-queen facade melts. Gage uncovers the vulnerable, tender woman beneath and wants more...which is fine, as long as it's not *too* much more. He's made a pact never to marry, and he's determined to see it through no matter how much he cares about Andy.

Too bad his heart has other plans.

Happy reading!

Jessica Lemmon

Learn more about the books at jessicalemmon.com.

Follow me on Instagram, @jlemmony.

JESSICA LEMMON

—

TEMPORARY TO TEMPTED

Recycling programs
for this product may
not exist in your area.

ISBN-13: 978-1-335-60357-9

Temporary to Tempted

Printed in U.S.A.

A former job-hopper, **Jessica Lemmon** resides in Ohio with her husband and rescue dog. She holds a degree in graphic design currently gathering dust in an impressive frame. When she's not writing supersexy heroes, she can be found cooking, drawing, drinking coffee (okay, wine) and eating potato chips. She firmly believes God gifts us with talents for a purpose, and with His help, you can create the life you want.

Jessica is a social media junkie who loves to hear from readers. You can learn more at jessicalemmon.com.

Books by Jessica Lemmon

Harlequin Desire

Dallas Billionaires Club

Lone Star Lovers
A Snowbound Scandal
A Christmas Proposition

The Bachelor Pact

Best Friends, Secret Lovers
Temporary to Tempted

Visit her Author Profile page at Harlequin.com, or jessicalemmon.com, for more titles.

One

Prospect number seven was not going well.

Andrea Payne's eyelids drooped as Dr. Christopher Miller yammered on. At this rate hell would freeze solid and Satan would win a gold medal in figure skating before she found an appropriate plus-one for her sister's wedding.

Her sister Gwen was the second to last of the Payne women to marry, which left Andy dead last. Not that Andy had ever been anywhere near walking down a runner in a wedding gown, but this marriage would widen the gap already setting her apart from her married—and one soon-to-be married—sisters.

Years ago, when she'd moved to Seattle, Andy had set out to prove that she didn't need a boyfriend; didn't need anyone. She'd set out to prove that in business, *in life*, she could stand on her achievements and skills.

In her family, charm and poise were worth more than achievements, and for that she could blame her mother, former Miss Ohio Estelle Payne. Andy would settle for relationships with high-paying clients, thank you very much. There was a contract between them, after all. That was sort of like marriage.

She returned her attention to her date, boredom having set in a while ago. It was a shame he wasn't going to work out. On paper, Christopher was everything she was looking for in a date for her sister's wedding. He was a doctor, well-dressed, nice-looking and comfortable talking about himself.

Really comfortable.

"Anyway, I was able to help out a patient in his time of need, which is what this job is all about." He arched his eyebrows and pressed his lips together, trying to appear humble. "He was lucky I was there."

Womp.

She'd tried her ex-boyfriends first—a whopping total of three of them—over the last month and a half before resorting to a dating app that had resulted in three other duds and "lucky number seven," Christopher here.

She gulped down the last of her chardonnay and flagged the waitress for a refill. Her date never broke stride.

"It wasn't the first time I've been tasked with removing a mole, but it's never an easy fight, and far more dangerous than anyone would imagine."

She sucked in air through her nose and plastered on what she hoped was a genial smile while surreptitiously checking out her surroundings. She'd noticed a trio at the bar earlier, and her attention returned there again. A guy and a girl who hadn't taken their eyes off each other and another guy who was there as a third wheel but didn't seem particularly bothered by it. She'd assumed he was waiting for his date while he had drinks with the couple, but then Andy noticed him flirting with the bartender. Maybe she was his girlfriend, though nothing between them hinted that they knew each other on an intimate level.

People-watching was one of Andy's favorite pastimes. She enjoyed making up stories about strangers, testing her observation skills. She only wished there was a way she could find out if she was right about her instincts.

The single guy—a gut call—at the bar was handsome in an earthy way, his light brown hair winding into curls here and there like it was in need of a trim, his shadowed beard a far cry from Christopher's sharply shaven jawline. Where Christopher resembled a firm pillar in a Brooks Brothers suit, the guy at the bar was in an approachable button-down pale-blue-and-white checked shirt, his tie—if there'd ever been one—long since tossed, and the sleeves cuffed and pushed to his elbows. He was drinking a bottle of beer, an expensive IPA if she wasn't mistaken, and that made her like him more.

"Andy?"

She jerked her attention to Christopher, who was a dark-haired, poor man's version of Chris Hemsworth. Not bad for a girl who was desperately seeking a date, but something about the good doctor was bothering her. Particularly that he was full of crap. Brimming with it, in fact.

How would she tolerate the entirety of a four-day wedding with him?

"Lost you there." He smirked and then continued the story of his latest medical triumph, talking down to her as if she still held her first job working part-time at a perfume counter. Not that he'd know what she did for a living. He never asked. If this bozo knew who he was trying to impress, he'd shut his mouth like a sprung bear trap.

She wondered what ole Christopher would say if he knew she was *the* Andy Payne, master of marketers. Sultan of sales. The oft-sought-after, rarely duplicated expert who was essentially a puff of smoke.

Everyone thought she was a man...on paper. She'd kept her identity a secret from everyone—including the many publications who'd interviewed her.

The New York Times.

Forbes.

Fortune.

That random mention in *Entertainment Weekly.*

Andy Payne was known for whipping companies into shape, and throughout her illustrious five-year career she'd managed to garner the attention of others with a clean black-and-white website and zero personal or identifying information about herself. When she showed up at the company, they knew on sight that she was a woman, but by then they were under her spell...and they'd signed a nondisclosure agreement.

Mostly she worked with men and, as she'd experienced in her first attempt at beginning a business as Andrea Anderson (last name chosen for alliteration), complete with a mauve and silver website filled with flowery words and cursive fonts, male clients didn't want to pay her what she was worth.

Enter her new identity. Andrea was easily changed to Andy, and she used her real last name. She let her clients' assumptions that she was male work in her favor.

"…not that I need *another* house in Tahiti." Christopher offered a smug smile and leaned back in his chair. Apparently, that was her cue to swoon or something.

She'd wasted enough time. First on her exes and now on the Find Love app. The wedding was in two weeks and she didn't have time for another round of failed interviews disguised as dates.

Andy hated to admit it, but in a deep dark corner of her heart she longed to be more like her sisters. She desired praise and approval from her mother. She wanted not necessarily to "fit in" but she would love not to *stand out*. In this case that meant appearing happily coupled off and avoiding needling observations from family members like that cousin at her sister Carroll's wedding.

I wish I was brave enough to show up at a wedding alone. If I didn't have a date, I would've just stayed home.

It wasn't enough to have a cardboard stand-in by her side, no, no. Andy needed to impress. Ideally her date could thwart those sorts of comments before they started.

Sadly, as impressive as Christopher believed he was, he wouldn't cut it as a proper wedding date.

Still. He was all she had. Time to get real.

"Christopher. I selected your profile because I

need a date for my sister's wedding. The gig is three nights, four days in amazing and luxurious Crown, Ohio. Your airfare will be covered and your hotel room will be separate, but also covered. You will be tasked with being my date, pretending to find everything I say amusing, and impressing my mother and father. You're skilled at bragging about how great you are but I will also need you to recognize that I'm in the room if we have any hope of pulling this off. Are you up for the mission I've presented you, or do you want to call it a night?"

He watched her carefully, an uncertain look on his face. "Are you— You're serious."

"As a heart attack. Which I hear you know a lot about."

"You want me to pretend to be your boyfriend."

"Yes."

"At a wedding."

"Yes."

He leaned forward and squinted one eye, his lips pursing as if deciding if the trip to Ohio would be worth his time, energy and effort.

Andy's palms were sweating. Not because she was excited by the doctor, but because her search might finally be over.

Then the idiot blurted, "Do we at least get to fuck?"

Yeah. They were *so* done.

"Good night, Christopher. I'll take care of the check."

"Wait, Andy—"

She tossed twenty bucks on the table to cover their drinks and marched to the ladies' room. The money would cover the single drink they'd each had and then she could go home and—

And what?

She was flat out of solutions. She had no close guy friends she could ask. Hell, she had no close girl-friends who might help her make a plan. What she had was money and prestige.

Just the thought of showing up at Gwen's wedding alone pissed her off. She refused to fail. It wasn't in her nature. Plus there was one other itty-bitty reason why showing up with a date was preferable.

One of her ex-boyfriends had been invited. She'd stooped low enough to call, which was bad enough, but then she learned that he was dating Gwen's best friend who was in the wedding. So that was gross.

Matthew Higgins had greeted her like no time had passed since they parted. *Well, well, well. If it isn't her royal highness.*

The Ice Queen. That was her.

Thank God she hadn't asked him to be her date. She'd played it off like she'd simply thought of him out of the blue and wanted to "catch up" and then ended the call before she died of humiliation.

At the double sink, she dug through her purse for her lip gloss, which evidently she'd neglected to pack in her clutch. She sighed in defeat. It'd been a long month.

A long *life*.

Around the time she'd dated Matt, she'd been sure she'd wind up marrying eventually. Until he repeat-edly teased her about her lack of warmth. She wasn't enough for him, and as much as she wished she could refute that, she'd also seen evidence in her family of what she was lacking. She wasn't as bubbly as Gwen. She wasn't as bold as Kelli. She wasn't as stylish as Ness. She wasn't as athletic as Carroll. As one of five girls in the Payne family, Andy was the unofficial black sheep. She'd just as soon not draw even more attention to their differences by becoming the last single one. Yet here she was.

For all the confidence and kick-ass-ness she possessed at work, she didn't want to be singled out or excluded from couples' activities.

Plus, nothing chapped her ass more than giving up.

She peeked out of a crack in the swinging door of the ladies' restroom to watch Christopher exit the bar. *Thank God.* Also, her twenty was still on the table, which was a plus. The last guy had taken her money and left, and she'd had to pay the waitress again.

There were no good men left in this city.

In the *world.*

"I can't catch another bouquet without a date," she whispered to herself. As humiliating as it was to catch the blasted thing—that her sisters always aimed her way—nothing was more humiliating than returning to the table with the flowers in hand and no date in sight. Guests always looked on in pity, as if she was going to die alone.

Her gaze snagged on the attractive guy at the bar and her back straightened with determination. If she was right about her observations, he was single. He was also sort of flirting with the bartender which hopefully meant he was looking.

Approaching him would be a random shot, but so had approaching every other guy she'd been out with. Maybe instead of taking home the cute bartender, he'd agree to bail out the too-serious, frosty, desperate-for-a-wedding-date single woman hiding in the ladies' room.

Probably not.

But Andy wasn't a failure.

She wouldn't *allow* failure.

She stepped from the restroom and spotted him—alone. The guy with the attractive facial hair and almost boyish curls. Except everything about the sculpted jaw and rounded shoulders screamed *man*. He was alone. Which meant the couple he'd been with had gone elsewhere.

Now was her chance.

Maybe her last chance.

"Money," she muttered.

She didn't have time for a get-to-know-you chat followed by the prospect of a date followed by her warming up to mention, "Hey, so my sister is getting married in two weeks…" She had to cut through the small talk and arrow straight to the point. Cash would make that a hell of a lot easier. She opened her clutch to count her credit cards. Five. That should be enough.

She rounded the corner to the ATM at the back of the bar, a plan in mind and a glass of good chardonnay in her belly.

She would take the simple approach and ask him if she could pay him to come with her to Ohio. Enough with faux dating and weighing the odds. She needed a date, and hopefully this guy needed a couple grand.

On a mission, she slid the first of five credit cards into the machine and punched the withdrawal button.

She would find a date to Gwen's wedding.

And she would find him tonight.

Two

Gage Fleming finished off his IPA and tipped the bottle's neck at the bartender. "I'll take the check when you have a second."

Seattle had come out of a long winter and cool spring, and was now firmly entrenched in summer. The energy was different during the hot months. The skirts were shorter and the nights were longer, and for him, the workdays were longer, too. He hadn't left his desk until well after seven thirty—hadn't gotten here until well after eight thirty. Given the hellacious week he'd had at the office, it didn't surprise him that he wasn't as upbeat as usual.

"Sure thing." Shelly was petite, wearing a ball cap with her ponytail sticking out of the back. Her lashes were thick, and her lips were shiny with gloss. Cute as she was, he didn't plan on asking her out. Even though she was his type, from her shapely calves to her low-cut V-necked T-shirt with the bar's gold-and-red emblem on it. Even though she'd been offering her smiles freely and borderline flirting back with him, Gage wasn't feeling it.

His best buddy Flynn and Sabrina, his other best buddy turned Flynn's girlfriend, had taken off a few minutes ago. Gage hung around at From Afar, finishing his beer after a long week and what felt like a longer workday.

He'd been friends with Flynn, Sabrina and Reid—who wasn't in the country at the moment—since college. Sabrina being in the mix was nothing new. Her being in love with Flynn and vice versa: totally new.

Gage had said yes to the after-work beer, not thinking it'd be any different than any other hangout they'd had before. It had been different, though, since the couple couldn't keep their hands or eyes on anything in the room but each other. But he couldn't begrudge his friends. A few months back, Flynn and Sabrina had slipped from the friend zone to the in-zone. Flynn was the happiest he'd been in a long while.

"Here you go, sweetheart." The cute blonde winked at him and moved away to greet another patron.

If he wasn't mistaken, that lifting feeling in his chest was relief at his decision not to dance the dance with her. Flirting was easy—hell, second nature—to him. Asking her out wouldn't be an issue. He had it down. He'd heard yes more times than no, and often heard "Yes!" shouted with exuberance later the same night in his bed.

Over the past few weeks, however, he'd noticed he was tired of the game. Going out on a few dates, a round or three of spectacular sex (or *okay* sex—but even okay sex was pretty damn good), and then finding his way out before things progressed to anything serious… If they got that far. Lately, he'd grown tired of the awkward parting in the middle of the night or the next morning. Tired of the walk of shame.

Thirty years old was too young to be this jaded.

You're just tired after a long week. Don't analyze it to death.

He leaned forward to pull his wallet from his back pocket, ready to pay and take his gloomy self home, when he noticed a stunning vision striding toward him. He froze, the scene unfolding in slow motion.

Strawberry blond hair washed over slim shoulders in a waterfall of color, bright against the narrow black sheath dress draped over her slender form. Electric blue eyes flashed with determination. She was long-limbed, her walk confident, and her full pink mouth was set in a firm, unsmiling line. One eyebrow was arched and she homed in on him like he was the target and she was a missile.

With his next breath, his libido returned. Lust slammed into his solar plexus and dried out his mouth.

Which made no sense.

In those heels, in that dress and with no smile to speak of, it was obvious he was in the presence of a way-too-serious woman. He'd had a close call with a woman like this one in his past, and he'd since decided that cute, bubbly bartenders were more his style.

Even so. Intrigued and more than a bit curious, he shoved his wallet back into his pocket when it became clear that this striking woman was coming right for him.

This one, he'd dance with. If only to shake things up a bit.

He'd buy her a drink, turn on the Fleming charm and see what happened. It'd been a while since a woman had snagged this much of his attention. Whether it was the strawberry blonde's determination or the set of her small shoulders, he couldn't be sure, but he couldn't tear his eyes off her. How could anyone look that damned delicate and at the same time like she ate nails for breakfast?

He didn't know. But he was going to find out. Something told him that she'd be worth it, no matter the cost.

"Shelly, I'll have another IPA after all," he said to the bartender, and as the strawberry blonde placed a manicured hand on the back of the bar stool next to him, he smoothly added, "and whatever she's having."

"You got it." Shelly dipped her chin at the strawberry blonde. "What'll it be?"

Strawberry yanked her gaze from Gage, her expression almost shocked that the bartender was talking to her. "Um. Chardonnay."

Shelly fetched their drinks and Gage turned to greet his guest, pulling the stool out for her to sit.

"No. Thanks," she replied coolly, almost like the "thanks" part was an afterthought.

Instinct told him that she wasn't as cool and calm as she pretended to be. If she was actually the man-eater she portrayed, she'd look him in the eye right now. Instead, she appeared to be steeling herself for some sort of proposition. Maybe she'd had a bad breakup, needed a little rebound.

That he could do.

"Can't enjoy your chardonnay without having a seat," he replied easily, patting the stool with one hand. Her eyebrows slammed down over her pert nose and she pegged him with an expression that bordered on fury.

A *zap!* hit him low in the gut. A warning drowned out by intense curiosity.

Let's tangle, honey.

A glass of chardonnay and a bottle of beer appeared in front of him, and without breaking away from her fiery blue gaze, he handed over the wine. Strawberry's nostrils flared, but she took the glass, tipped it to her lips and had sucked down a third of it by the time he'd lifted his bottle.

Yep. She was definitely here on a mission.

She set the glass down with a loud *clink.* "I'll pay you two thousand dollars to spend a weekend with me."

Gage lowered his beer without taking a sip. His mouth was poised to say the word *what* but he didn't have a chance to say anything before she was opening her purse and showing him the contents. Stacks of twenties were packed into it, facing every which way like she'd robbed a convenience store before propositioning him.

"I'm attending a destination wedding in the Midwest in two weeks. Your flight and separate room will be paid in full. I'll give you two thousand dollars to go with me."

Just as he'd settled on the notion that this beauti-

ful creature was certifiably insane, a flicker of doubt
lit her expressive eyes.

"I need you to pretend to be my boyfriend for
the duration. I know Ohio doesn't sound scenic, but
Crown is a beautiful, quaint town. And there will be
food," she added with a touch of desperation. "Really good food."

Her throat moved as she swallowed thickly, her
outer layer of surety and confidence flaking away.

Seemed he was right about her being on a mission, but damn, he'd been wrong about her not being
a man-eater. She was so similar to his ex, he wouldn't
be surprised if she pulled off a mask to reveal Laura
herself.

He took a long slug of his beer and then swiped
his tongue over his bottom lip. This woman was either crazy or desperate or both. Figured. He should've
known a woman this beautiful would be nuttier than
a sack of trail mix.

"Well?" Her eyebrow arched again, her too-serious
expression snapping seamlessly into place. "I don't
have much time, so I'd appreciate an answer."

Was she for real?

He'd never imagined she'd march over here and
demand to…to…*hire him* to be her date, let alone expect him to agree without so much as a casual intro-
duction. For all he knew, she would lure him in with
promises and then steal his identity.

Or my kidneys.

The answer was an easy no, but he wouldn't let
her off the hook without making her explain first. He
opened the edge of her purse with his index finger

so he could examine the cash inside as he pretended to consider her offer.

"How will payment work? You just hand me all the money in your purse and then I give you my phone number?"

"No. Of course not." She snatched her bag out of his reach. "Then I'd have no guarantee you'd show up. I'd give it to you at the wedding."

"Why would I clear my weekend plans and fly with you to Ohio on a promise of two thousand dollars if I don't have any of it?"

A frown muddled her pretty face. "You can have half. But I need your phone number. And your address. And your word."

Unbelievably gorgeous and absolutely crackers. It was a shame.

"But I need your answer now."

"Right now." His gaze locked on her pink mouth and he had a moment of regret for not getting to have a taste of her lips. To feel how silky that red hair was against his fingertips. He lifted his beer bottle, delaying. The kissing and fingers in her hair were an impossibility but his curiosity to watch her reaction still burned. He was trying to decide what she would do when he said no. Would she slap him or scream at him or run from the bar?

"Yes, now," she said through her teeth.

Damn. Maybe he could convince her to stick around after he shot her down.

"I can't help you out, Strawberry. I don't particularly like the Midwest. And despite what first impression I must've given you, I don't need two thousand dollars. But if you'd like to finish your wine—"

That long swath of hair flicked as she turned on her heel and tromped toward the exit. Option C it was. She left behind a plume of softly scented perfume and a fantasy that lasted the rest of the week. One about long, silky hair and a parted pink mouth. About her beneath him naked atop those bills scattered over his bed...

Whoever she was, she left an impression. The way looking at the sun left bright light burning behind his lids for a while.

Gage turned back to his beer. Even though Strawberry was a little nutty, he honestly hoped she found a date to that wedding in Ohio.

Three

"Today's the day."

Gage rubbed his hands together and then fired up the espresso machine in the executive break room.

"What day's that?" Reid, back from his recent trip home to London, asked.

"The day that Andy Payne guy comes to save Gage's rear end," Sabrina answered as she tipped the half-and-half into her mug.

"Not *my* rear. *Our* rears," Gage corrected. "This is going to help boost sales, yes, but this will also take some of the pressure off Flynn." He grinned at Sabrina. "You're welcome."

Last year Gage had come up with the perfect solution for the senior staff at Monarch Consulting, who had been giving Flynn holy hell. When Flynn's father died, leaving Flynn in charge of the company, a

lot of the men and women who were used to the way
Emmons had run things hadn't taken too kindly to
Flynn. Gage's suggestion—*brilliant* suggestion—
was to focus on sales, create a huge boom in business, which would satisfy shaky investors and give
a needed boost to everyone's bonuses. It was hard to
complain when extra money rolled in.

"Oh, I'm welcome, am I?" Sabrina chuckled.

"If it's gratitude you want, mate, just ask," Reid
commented.

Gage didn't want gratitude, but he did want results. The company had felt as if it was teetering
on a foundation of marbles last year and he hadn't
liked it at all. Monarch Consulting was the workplace
Gage had called home since college. He didn't want
to work anywhere else. He loved what he did, loved
his friends and in no way wanted to end up working
at a fish hatchery like his parents. Flynn's success as
president ensured all of their successes.

Flynn stepped into the room, picking up on the
conversation. "Let me guess. You have your panties in a wad of excitement over the arrival of the guy
made of smoke?"

The guy who was the key to stabilizing Monarch,
bringing in extra money *and* a business boom?

Hell, yes.

Andy Payne was a fixer of sorts who was known
for not being known. He'd been interviewed but never
filmed, and his About page was devoid of a photo or
any description of him as a person. Gage wasn't sure
if he bought into the hero-worship BS surrounding
Andy Payne's reputation, but the man's results were

rock solid. Every employee had signed nondisclosure documents before Payne's arrival.

Plus, if this Andy guy was half as good in person as he was on paper, Monarch would be set and Flynn's leadership would go unchallenged. Succeeding was the only option. Gage had never taken a backwards step since he'd set foot in Monarch and he wouldn't start now. He had goals to double the company's revenue, and making his sales department shine would tuck in nicely with that goal.

It was a big goal, but Andy Payne was a big deal. With his help there wasn't anything standing in Gage's way.

Andy strolled into the Monarch building wearing her best suit. Bone-colored, with a silky black cami under the jacket, her Jimmy Choos an easy-to-navigate height. She had to work in them, after all.

She'd never understood any woman's desire to sacrifice form for comfort. She wasn't a fan of compromise.

Andy hadn't accepted her fate from the weekend, either. Yes, she'd quit the dating app that'd been a total waste of resources. And, yes, she had felt the sting of embarrassment about propositioning a handsome stranger at a bar, but that didn't mean her search was over. There was still a chance, though slim, to find a stand-in date. Maybe she would meet a nice guy on her way out of this very building. Or maybe at the resort.

Doubt pushed itself forward but she fervently ignored it. Instead she allowed herself to feel the familiar thrum of excitement as she rode the elevator up to the executive floor. First days were her *favorite*.

She'd done extensive research on Monarch, noting that the only photo of the staff was one gathered outside the front of this very building, their faces tiny and nondescript. If businesses were to entrust Monarch with their well-being, they needed to see the trustworthy faces who worked here.

Unlike most businesses, Andy had worked hard to keep her identity under wraps. She had no qualms about pulling a bait and switch on day one. By then everyone was invested and her reputation had preceded her. She never blatantly led her clients to believe Andy Payne was male, but much like the assumption that a surgeon was always a man, so, too, was one made that the wild success of her Fortune 500 business must be attributed to someone with a penis instead of a pair of breasts.

The pay gap that existed between men and women didn't exist for her, thanks to her subterfuge. Her clients paid what was asked, and it was too late to pull the plug once the contracts were signed. She wouldn't apologize for it.

She was absolutely worth it.

She was the best at what she did and she endeavored to leave every business better than she'd found it. Monarch was going to be another link in a long chain of satisfied customers.

With a flip of her hair she exited the elevator on the executive floor. Three huge offices with glass walls stood empty, a front desk staffed with a young blonde woman in front of one of them. Andy was early, so probably the executives hadn't come out of the coffee or break room yet. Muted voices and laughter came from an unseen room in the back.

One of those voices likely belonged to Gage, the senior sales executive who'd hired her.

"May I help you?" the assistant asked.

Andy addressed her by her name, advertised on the nameplate on the front of her desk. "Hello, Yasmine. Andy Payne for Gage Fleming."

"Andy Payne?"

"That's me." She grinned.

"Oh, of course, Ms. Payne. We have you set up in the conference room as you requested."

Yasmine quickly recovered from her surprise at discovering that Andy was a woman. Good for her.

In the conference room, Yasmine pointed out the projector and offered to fetch Andy an espresso.

"Americano, if you can."

The other woman dipped her chin in affirmation and left.

Andy unloaded her bag on the table—a rigorous sales plan and a dossier on Monarch minus details on the man she was meeting, since she'd learned virtually nothing about him via the website.

Done right, they could implement her suggested changes in the week and a half she had before she would have to fly to Ohio for Gwen's wedding.

Gag. Just the thought of that bit of unfinished business rankled her.

But Gage Fleming had hired Andy on her merits at business, not based on whether or not she was datable. She shoved aside all thoughts of the wedding and focused on what she did most—what she did *best*—fixing companies.

* * *

Flynn and Sabrina left the haven of the break room, Gage and Reid following behind. On their walk to their offices, Gage asked Reid, "How was your trip?"

His British friend, coffee mug lifted, grinned. "Grand."

"Because of…"

"Suzie Daniels. A pretty American in a foreign land who needed companionship from a local who was willing to show her a good time." Reid rested his palm over his heart. "I showed her repeatedly. Lucky lady."

Gage had to chuckle. Reid was a playboy and a half, but he was also a nice guy. No doubt Suzie Daniels had kissed him farewell and hadn't regretted a single minute of their time together. Gage hadn't been as fortunate with his past hookups. He must throw off a serious boyfriend vibe. The women he dated always wanted more, always wanted it too quickly and weren't happy when he declined. The last woman he dated had told him he'd wasted her time and said she wished she'd never met him. Ouch.

"And your weekend?" Reid asked, stopping next to Gage's office.

"Went to From Afar with Flynn and Sabrina on Friday night for a drink after work. After they left, the strangest thing…" Gage fell silent when he spotted a flash of red hair in the conference room. And when her head lifted slightly and he caught sight of her profile, he recognized her instantly.

She was the woman who'd attempted to buy him like a suit off a rack. The more he'd thought about that interaction the more it had bothered him. Not because he felt cheap or used, but because the beauty who'd invaded his dreams had truly believed the money was going to seal the deal with them. As if she didn't have enough confidence to strike up a conversation about what she needed, but instead felt the need to offer him cash.

"Holy hell." Gage grabbed Reid's arm and dragged him back into the hallway they'd just exited, Reid complaining since he'd sloshed coffee onto the carpet and narrowly missed his shoes. Gage had done a good job of spilling his own coffee on his shirt. Hot liquid burned through the pale blue button-down, and he swore.

"What just happened?" Reid shook coffee droplets off his fingers.

"She's stalking me." Gage scrubbed at his shirt with one hand.

"Who?"

Reid peered around the corner and Gage slunk farther into the hall. When he'd concluded that the redhead was "crackers," he'd thought he'd been half joking. Apparently, he hadn't.

"That's the woman I was just going to tell you about," Gage whispered, though there was no way she could hear him from the conference room. "She approached me at the bar Friday night and offered to pay me two grand to spend a weekend with her."

Reid's eyebrows lifted, wrinkling his brow. "And you said no." He stole another peek and regarded Gage dubiously. "Why?"

"Because she's insane?" That seemed the only reasonable explanation now.

"You're the insane one, my friend, if you didn't snap her up and have your way with her right there on the bar top. Hell, I wouldn't have charged her at all."

"The offer wasn't for sex. It was for me to fly to Ohio and attend a wedding. She wanted me to pretend to be seeing her or something."

"Oh." Reid's disappointment was obvious. "That's not the same thing at all."

"No. It's not." Gage returned to the break room and set his mug aside. He grabbed a dish towel and scrubbed at the coffee stain low on his shirt.

Reid wasn't far behind. "What's she doing here?"

"I have no idea."

"Gage?" Yasmine stepped into the break room. "Andy Payne is here to see you."

"Perfect timing." Gage gestured at his soiled shirt. "Tell him I'll be right out. Who's the redhead?"

Yasmine blinked. "Andy Payne."

"Andy Payne is the fixer, love," Reid told her gently. "We want to know who the vixen in the cream-colored suit is."

"Andy Payne," Yasmine repeated with slow insistence and enough confidence that Reid and Gage exchanged glances.

"*She's* Andy Payne?" Gage asked, still trying to wrap his head around the idea that the woman who approached him at the bar was the "guy" he'd hired to whip his sales team into shape.

"Surprising, right? How sexist are we?" Yasmine shrugged. "I thought Andy was going to be a dude, too."

Reid smiled to beat all. "I believe I'll go with you

to meet this Andy Payne, Gagey. Do bring up Friday for my benefit, yeah?"

"No," Gage growled, his head still spinning with the new information. "I'll go alone to meet...her."

As he exited the break room, he muttered, "Again."

Four

The projector was positioned, her laptop open and the PowerPoint presentation cued up.

Andy tidied the bound sales plans—one for her and one for Gage. She'd arranged herself at the head of the conference table and placed the report to her left elbow at the corner. She found it easier to coordinate a plan when they weren't facing each other from opposing sides.

Sometimes these meetings went smoothly, with the managers or CEOs who'd hired her easing into the adjustment as they learned that Andy Payne was the female currently introducing herself. Other times, they reacted angrily and accused her of pulling a fast one on them. Mostly it was the former.

They'd hired her for her expertise, and that was what she reminded them of when she arrived. She'd only had three men ever react poorly and had only ever lost one job because of it. The sexist bastard. No matter, her contract was ironclad and nonrefundable. She'd bought a weekend spa retreat with the money that particular time and had no qualms about enjoying her paid leave.

She sat on the edge of the padded chair and turned her head in time to see a man rapidly approaching the conference room. She recognized the scruffy jaw, the slight curl to the longish hair on top of his head…and the answering recognition in his caramel-brown eyes.

She stood slowly, feeling her jaw drop to the floor as he shut the conference room door behind him and looked down his nose at her. Although she wasn't that much shorter than him.

"*You're* Andy Payne," he said flatly.

Her mouth still agape, she managed a stunned nod. Warmth seeped from her cami, over her décolletage and up her neck. No doubt she was turning a stunning shade of pink while he watched her.

And he did watch her. Carefully. And unhappily.

As quickly as she could move, she slapped the lid closed on her laptop and yanked the cord free from the wall. "I'm—uh," she said as she hastily stacked the reports. "I have to…um…"

She yanked her bag off the chair but the strap caught, scattering the pages in her dossier on Monarch to the floor along with several pens, her cell phone charger and a tube of lipstick.

This was going well.

She crouched to the floor to sweep the contents of the bag back into it. "You must be Gage."

"In the flesh." He knelt next to her and picked up one of her pens that had fallen to the floor.

"I didn't know you were you when I approached you on Friday or I never would've done it," she said as she gathered her things. A lock of hair swept over her eye and she blew a puff of air from her lips to move it.

"You don't say." His eyebrows flinched slightly, but some of the anger simmered away, his expression almost bemused as his eyes roamed over her face.

He was stupidly attractive. Even more so in a suit. Even with a coffee stain on his shirt that looked fresh. That attraction was all the more reason why she couldn't stay another moment. She'd never be able to look him in the eye again after she'd… God…*offered to pay him* to be her date.

"I'll refund your money for the consultation contract." She snatched the pen from his hand and stood. He stood with her and the view of the rest of him was finer than it had appeared on Friday night. His muscular chest pressed the confines of his shirt, a dark blue tie in place and knotted just so. His slacks were navy as well, and a brown leather belt bisected his waist. His shoes matched—expensive and shiny.

"First you want to hire me, now you want to give me a refund. You offer to pay me an awful lot."

She blanched.

"And the hell you will." He folded his arms over his impressive chest. His unsmiling mouth pursed. "I hired you to do a job. You're not running out on me just because you—"

"Don't say it." Her eyes sank closed and she palmed one burning-hot cheek. Was it possible to die of humiliation? "I know what I did and I apologize." She reopened her eyes and turned them up to his. "Please tell me you didn't tell anyone about it?"

"I told my friend Reid. He works here. You'll meet him later."

"You told someone?" Her voice was edging along hysterical and she forced herself to calm down. "You could've kept that to yourself."

"Is that a joke? A gorgeous woman approaches me in a bar and I decide to stay one drink longer to get to know her and then she offers to pay me two grand for my companionship? It's a hell of a story, *Andy*."

He thought she was…gorgeous? And he'd wanted to get to know her?

It was far and wide two of the most flattering compliments she'd heard in a while.

"I didn't know you were *the* Andy Payne when I told him. I thought you'd tracked me down at work, and that you were going to… I don't know, try and reconvince me."

That was fair.

Why would he assume she was here for any other reason? She'd been on a mission to achieve her goal on Friday and had—incorrectly—assumed that when she ran from that bar, mentally vowing never to return, she wouldn't see Gage again.

She hadn't asked him his name, either.

"I wasn't myself that night. I was angry about my date not working out and then I noticed you—" She snapped her mouth closed before she accidentally said too much, and then rerouted the conversation. "This is no fault of yours. I'll go directly to my office from here and refund your money immediately." She added the laptop and reports to her bag and pulled it over her shoulder.

"No deal." He stepped in front of the door and blocked her path.

"Step aside, Mr. Fleming."

"Not going to happen, *Ms*. Payne." His nostrils flared as he pulled in a breath. "I hired you. You agreed to do a job. I know you're the best—I did my research. You've been cited as an asset by hundreds of companies, and I'm not letting you go because you made a mistake and now you're uncomfortable. We have a contract. I was told your fee was nonrefundable."

That was true. Normally. "I'll make an exception."

A warm, gentle palm landed on her upper arm. His voice was equally gentle when he said, "I don't want an exception. I want you to stay and double or triple our numbers like you promised. This is important."

His words were sincere. And a good reminder that she prided herself on her work ethic. She *never* let clients down. She worked tirelessly for them because their businesses mattered. Employees had families to care for, and when she made their companies more money, the companies in turn lined the pockets of those hardworking men and women. What she did wasn't about fattening up greedy CEOs. She did this work for the people. All of them.

And right now Gage looked like someone who needed her help.

"Did you find a date for the wedding yet?" he asked.

She blinked, stunned by the change of topic.

"I'll go," he said. "You stay here for the time you

promised and I'll go with you to Ohio to your sister's wedding."

"But—"

"I suspect you'll insist, so I'll let you take care of the room and flight, but you can keep the two grand." He dipped his chin in a show of sincerity. "Okay?"

As much as she hated to admit it, his offer was really, *really* tempting. She had to face reality, and the reality was that she was no closer to finding a date for Gwen's wedding than she was to sprouting wings and flying there on her own steam.

A bigger part of her was tempted simply because of Gage. He was attractive, and had found her attractive, and she wouldn't mind spending more time getting to know him. Of all the dates she'd set up in an attempt to find a companion for Gwen's wedding, Gage, from his warm brown eyes to his shiny leather shoes, was the only one who'd made her heart flutter. Dr. Christopher certainly hadn't wanted to get to know her better. He hadn't even had the decency to turn the money down.

Even so, she found herself answering, "I couldn't ask you to do that."

"Too bad. You already did, on Friday night. Now I'm accepting." He lifted her bag off her shoulder, his fingers leaving behind an imprint of heat she couldn't ignore. He set the bag on the conference room table, pulling her laptop out and extracting the reports, one of which had an ugly crease on the otherwise pristine cover.

What a metaphor for Andy herself right now. She'd come in here neat and poised and now felt more than a little bent.

He opened the laptop screen and took the wrinkled report and sat in his seat. She again considered refusing his offer. Her pride told her to bolt and never look back.

There was only one problem. She needed him.

Almost as much as he needed her.

Five

Gage had to hand it to her. Andy knew what she was doing.

A week later, he sat at a conference table with Flynn and Reid and his right-hand guy on his sales team, Bruce, reviewing the numbers. The numbers were good.

Really freaking good.

"Bonuses will look great this quarter," Bruce commented, his smile wide. A thirty-nine-year-old father of seventeen-year-old twins, he could use the extra money. Both of Bruce's daughters would be graduating and going to college soon.

"Share the good news," Gage told him. "That's all I have. Flynn? Reid? Anything?"

"Not on my end," Flynn said. "Just, good job."

Reid echoed the sentiment, shook Bruce's hand,

and then Bruce left the executive floor with some really good news for the sales team.

"She's as good as she claims," Flynn commented to Gage. "Andy."

"She is."

"And bloody fast," Reid commented. "I've never seen anyone swoop in and offer suggestions that work immediately."

"She's amazing," Gage admitted. She was also all business. She strode in here Monday through Friday to train, observe and then meet with Gage on her findings. He'd done some observing of his own—of her—and he couldn't escape the idea that she'd walled part of herself off.

Last week, when he'd walked into this very conference room, she hadn't been determined and all business. She'd been flustered and embarrassed. She'd been *human*. He liked witnessing that human side of her—the flush to her cheeks as her seriousness chipped away leaving her open vulnerability visible. She was able to get shit done, took no crap from anyone, and yet he'd noticed a shier, more withdrawn part of her.

"Are the two of you still on for the wedding arrangement?" Reid asked, a troublemaking twinkle in his eye.

"I agreed to help her out so she wouldn't walk. You'd have done the same thing. It's only a weekend."

Four days, technically, but he was trying to downplay it. He'd agreed so she wouldn't walk out, yes, but he'd also agreed because learning that the woman from the bar and Andy Payne were the same person had intrigued him in a way no other woman had in years. He wanted to cash in on his fantasy vision of her beneath him, sure, but he was also curious as hell why she felt the need to pay someone—him, specifically. She'd hinted that day in the conference room that there was something about him that had drawn her in. Why him? What had she seen across that bar that made her approach him?

In the time she'd spent at Monarch he still knew next to nothing about her. She was as uncrackable as a sealed safe. He still wasn't sure what he was supposed to "do" at her side at the wedding. What role was he to play other than a date who danced with her or fetched her a glass of champagne? He needed to find out, but in order to do that he had to get her out of Monarch and into an environment where she wasn't so…distant.

"She's not light and bubbly like the women you're used to seeing. Maybe a wedding will loosen her up." Reid stood.

"She's serious about her job but that's not a bad thing," Gage said in her defense. He rose from his chair and Flynn followed suit.

"It's not," Flynn agreed. "She's a hard-core professional. Does everything she says she's going to do, and follows through like a boss." The description sounded like Flynn himself.

"I was just pointing out that she's the opposite of the type of woman you gravitate toward." Reid narrowed his eyes. "Lately."

What Reid was not-so-subtly hinting at was that Andy was, at first glance, a lot like Gage's ex-fiancée.

He didn't want to talk about Laura any more than he wanted to bring up politics at a dinner party. He'd admired her strong work ethic and serious nature. In the end, he'd believed in them more than she had.

She'd broken the engagement, coldly stating that he wasn't enough like her. He had a case of the "toos." He was *too* likable, *too* fun and *too* easygoing. She'd claimed she needed someone "serious" about the future. The corrosion of that engagement was his biggest failure.

Gage hated failure.

He'd been sure that Andy was that same kind of woman—cold, calculating— until he'd witnessed her flustered. Seeing that chink in her armor had drawn him in rather than pushed him away. He hadn't completely understood it. After the hell Laura'd put him through he'd be smart not to pursue Andy at all.

But he'd never been one to back down from a challenge, and Gage sensed there was warmth and gentleness underneath Andy's rigid exterior that had yet to surface. The more of her flaws he exposed, the more he proved that the attraction wasn't some masochistic repeat of the past with Laura, but some new, fascinating layer to Andy herself.

He liked that she had an imperfect, human side that rarely showed, that she was a mystery waiting to be uncovered. That she didn't have it together 24/7. Plus she was downright sexy. If he found an opening to show her how sexy she was, he'd happily oblige.

Not that his agreeing to be Andy's wedding date had been totally magnanimous. He'd needed her to stay on at Monarch for both appearances and results, and a few days in Ohio seemed a small price to pay.

Flynn and Sabrina had left the office around five. Now that Flynn had a girlfriend in Sabrina, he rarely worked as late as he had before. Reid had a date as well, so he'd packed up and followed them out. That left Gage alone in the executive corner of the office, waiting at his desk for Andy's daily report, which came at around 5:30 p.m.

She strolled in wearing her office attire of black pants, low shoes and a silky white shirt. Her gold jewelry was simple and understated, except for the large-faced watch, which she glanced down at before she entered.

Mouth a flat line, determination in her eyes, she stalked toward him like a hungry lioness. Much like the first time he'd seen her, he watched her approach with an even mix of intrigue and attraction.

Could he uncover the fun, flirty girl under that armor? Was there one?

"Your team is exceptional, Gage," she said, skipping over a greeting. "Which is in no small part thanks to you being a dedicated, earnest leader."

His eyebrows lifted at the compliment he wasn't expecting. But then she spoke again and made it obvious that she'd come in here with an agenda.

"I have an itinerary, your plane ticket and a few other details to cover for this weekend's wedding if you're available for a quick rundown. I know it's last-minute, but I've been busy."

All business, he thought with a smile. He'd always enjoyed a challenge but, he was realizing, lately he'd pursued challenges professionally rather than personally. He hadn't chased women who'd challenged him since Laura left. Then again, Andy had been the only one who'd tempted him to do so since.

"What are you doing right now?" he asked her.

"Now?" Her eyes widened slightly.

"Yeah. Now. Dinner?"

She shook her head like what he was saying didn't compute.

"Are you hungry?" he pressed.

"Yes."

"Are you busy right now?"

"I'm always busy."

He waited.

She shrugged and affected an *unaffected* expression. "Fine."

"Great. I'll drive."

"Where are we going?"

"Why? Are you picky? Have allergies?"

"No." She frowned.

"Then don't worry about it." He winked, enjoying throwing her off-kilter.

He needed a little more fun in his life and Andy *definitely* needed a little more fun in her life. He liked that she seemed unused to a man strong enough or willing enough to take her on. He just liked her, dammit, though he wasn't yet sure why he liked her this much.

In the immediate seconds following Gage's invitation to dinner, Andy wanted to blurt out that she needed to change first. Thankfully she resisted that very female urge. Just because Gage was playing her date at the wedding didn't mean he was one tonight. She would pretend they were an item, enjoy the reprieve from her family's judgment, and relish showing up an old ex-boyfriend who thought she'd been carved from a block of ice. But she'd keep the boundary lines very clear in her head. Gage had agreed to be her date for one reason: because he'd needed her expertise at work.

Without something to gain, he wasn't interested in her—he'd turned her down that night in the bar, after all.

Still, being around him was a rare exception she admitted she was tempted to enjoy. She was a hard sell to any man—even without the offer to pay him. A man who was both professional *and* not intimidated by her success was a rare commodity. Like finding a unicorn.

Even though her arrangement with Gage wouldn't last any longer than her sister's reception, Andy figured it'd be good to get to know him so that her family wouldn't suspect she'd bribed him to come. The only thing more humiliating than showing up at her sister's wedding with a fake date would be everyone learning that she was faking it.

But the stray thought about changing for dinner with Gage had rocked her. Why would she care what he thought of her appearance if they weren't doing this for real? She'd long ago accepted that a forever-and-ever relationship wasn't going to happen, and yet something about Gage—about his charm and kindness—made a small part of her wish this was real.

He wasn't intimidated by her. If anything, the more prickly she was, the more laid-back he seemed to become. Laid-back and yet more than a little commanding.

It was an odd mix. She didn't have him figured out yet.

Which was why she'd spent the weekend writing

up the wedding itinerary and finalizing the details of their arrangement. She needed to get them on the same page, and fast, if they had any prayer of pulling this off.

At least she'd have Gage by her side when she inevitably bumped into her ex-boyfriend Matthew. The thought of him smugly pointing out that she was as frigid as she'd always been irritated her.

She wished she didn't care. Wished she didn't want to rub her ex's nose in her business success—*and* her relationship success—in spite of the label he'd given her years ago. But she did.

She was only human, after all.

Gage chose a fairly high-end restaurant downtown for dinner. With its black tablecloths and dim lighting, candles in the center of the table and à la carte menu, it was a touch more romantic than she'd counted on. Maybe she should've insisted on going home to change rather than continue in her casual work attire—if only to fit in with the well-coiffed crowd.

The host pulled her chair out for her and she sat, lifting the menu to study the options.

"Wine, Andy?" Gage asked. "Or should I call you something else in public to protect your secret identity? Bruce Wayne, maybe."

"Ha-ha." She lowered the menu to give him a slow blink. "I'll stick with sparkling water, but thank you."

When their waiter came by, Gage ordered a bottle of Cabernet alongside her sparkling water.

"We never finished the first drink we had together," he pointed out. "Tonight would feel stuffy if we didn't indulge."

She did indulge—one glass had the rigors of her workday melting off her shoulders like butter in the hot sun. There was something about Gage that brought out her relaxed side. Maybe it was his own casual attitude. How he could wear a suit in a fancy restaurant as well as he did and still smile as genially as if they were lounging on his sofa together…it was beyond her.

Andy had accepted that she simply wasn't the fun, carefree type. Outside of this agreement with Gage, she couldn't imagine snagging his attention. And yet being around him felt strangely comfortable— which was probably why she didn't hang around him at work. She didn't want to be unduly comfortable and slip up—she had a job to do. She couldn't pretend to be able to live up to his fun, easy-going standards. That simply wasn't who she was. Except that she needed to be *really* comfortable around him at Gwen's wedding for this charade to work.

After they'd eaten their dinners, they settled in to finish off the wine, Gage resting one masculine hand on the rim of his glass. He lifted it the same way and gestured to her with the stem.

"Let's hear the plan."

Was it any wonder he was fantastic at his job? He exuded confidence and charm, and if she were a twitchy CEO in search of a consulting firm, she'd buy an air conditioner from Gage in the wintertime. Just to urge forth that sincere, pleased smile.

To please him in general.

That thought brought forth another, one of pleasing him in a physical way. With her touch, with her kiss.

Alarming, since Andy had just tasked herself with

keeping things between them strictly professional. Why did he have to be so damned attractive? Why did he have to be so damned likeable? Why did he act as if he liked her so much in return? That was the real lure. He seemed to like her just as she was— prickly and unapproachable, rigid and serious. She really wished he'd have let her pay him so the lines weren't so blurry.

"I emailed you an itinerary," she told him, firmly setting the conversation back on solid ground.

"When?"

"In the car on the drive over. Do you want to cue it up so we can review it together? It covers the schedule in detail, including what time each event starts and where we'll be staying. I left your airline ticket at my apartment but I can bring it to Monarch tomorrow."

"Those aren't the kinds of details I need from you, Andy."

"No?" She wasn't sure what else there was. Unless… "I did type up a detailed family member list, but that seemed like overpreparing. If you and I were really dating, you wouldn't necessarily remember all their names."

"Those aren't the details I need, either." He shook his head, took a sip from his wine and swallowed.

When his tongue stroked his lip to catch a wayward crimson drop, she pressed her knees together under the table. His mouth might be the most distracting part about him.

"I need to know," that mouth said, lazily pronouncing each syllable, "how much physical affection you'd like from me."

Six

"Hold your hand. Put my palm on your lower back. Those are both givens. But what about kissing? How much? How often? How *deep*?"

Gage watched Andy carefully as he doled out each option as if on a menu like the one they'd ordered from tonight. He enjoyed the surprise rounding her wide blue eyes as much as the flush creeping along her fair skin. "When we're at dinner, would you like me to feed you a bite, kiss your hand, gaze longingly into your eyes?"

"Is any of that necessary?" She sounded worried that it might be.

"Not unless we're trying to make someone jealous. In which case—very necessary. But if you have a fairly reserved family, I'll keep the touching to a minimum."

Clearly befuddled, she shakily lifted her wine and polished off the glass. He smoothly refilled it, happy to ply her with enough alcohol to have her tell him the truth. He ignored the frisson of discomfort at pursuing Andy so doggedly. She'd caught his attention. She had his admiration. Why not pursue something physical with her? It wasn't as if he'd allow himself to get in as deeply as he had with Laura. That situation had been one and done, and he'd learned not to tempt fate.

He'd recommitted to the bachelor pact with Flynn and Reid for a reason: Gage would never again consider marriage.

Flynn had backed out of the pact after he and Sabrina had obliterated the just-friends boundary, but Sabrina was the ultimate exception. She was one of their own—who better to settle down with Flynn than the one woman who would never, ever betray him?

Gage's motivation was different. He'd been thoroughly blinded by his love for Laura. He'd felt like a complete jackass for overlooking her cold-hearted demeanor, and had assumed their physical attraction and professional goals were enough to sustain a life together. He'd been young, and stupid, and all along she'd been more concerned about his financial potential than a stable marriage. After they imploded, he'd set out to make ten times as much money as she'd earn in her lifetime just to prove her wrong.

Over the years his drive became less and less about proving Laura wrong. Gage had grown to love success, and was a damn good leader. His strengths had served him well and he'd helped his best friend build a company and a sales team they could all be proud of.

Gage was a different person now than he was when he'd been engaged to Laura. Just because Andy had a similar passion for achievement was no reason to ignore the ninety-foot flames between them whenever she was near. That siren's wail he'd heard in his head was nothing more than a false alarm, concocted by the former version of himself.

"Why do you need a date for the wedding?" he asked, curious. "Why not go alone?"

"I've caught three bouquets and I don't want to catch a fourth," she answered. Strangely.

"Pardon?"

"I have four sisters. Three of them are happily married and the fourth is about to be. I don't want to catch Gwen's bouquet. If I go alone and am called to the dance floor, then Gwen will inevitably aim that bouquet right for me…" She shuddered like this was the worst fate that could befall her.

"I'm guessing not because you have an aversion to flowers?"

Andy shook her head.

"You don't want the attention?"

"I don't want the attention for being single. It's a running joke in my family."

He couldn't believe she'd admitted that much. The wine must be working. He didn't dare interrupt in case she had more to say. Turned out she did.

"I have a reputation as a hard-ass. Shocking, I know." She added a self-deprecating eye roll that he'd have found adorable if he didn't believe she was sincere. "I've never had a date to one of my sister's weddings. I'm pretty sure they think I live this lonely, pathetic existence married to my work or whatever."

"Did you date much when you lived in Ohio?"

"A few serious relationships that fizzled out. They didn't last and when we split I mostly felt relieved. One of them will be there, by the way." She chucked back the last inch of wine and waved her glass for a refill.

Gage obliged her.

"His name's Matthew," she snarled. "When we broke up he told me I'd die alone. I don't want him to know he was right."

"You're far from death's door, Andy."

"I'm not interested in permanence," she stated, a flicker of challenge in her eyes. He wouldn't argue.

"On that we agree." He clinked his glass with hers. Unbeknownst to her, she'd given him an angle to work with. "Aside from my being your arm candy—" her impish smile emerged and brought forth an answering one of his own "—you'd like to show up this Matthew guy."

"I don't need to show him up." Bright eyes pegged him, truth in their cobalt depths. "I just don't want him to know he's won."

Gage didn't like that the bastard had coldly stated that Andy would spend her life alone any more than he liked the idea of her believing that her ex was right.

"We'll play it by ear." He reached across the table and offered a hand—handshake-style since he wasn't sure how she'd react to a more intimate touch. But when she placed her palm against his, he held onto her hand gently and made a promise he knew he'd keep. "You asked the right guy to be your wedding date, Andy. I won't let you down."

* * *

Gage had admitted during the flight that he didn't know much about Ohio. He'd told her that he knew there was a lot of corn, and that it was in the Midwest. Ohio wasn't *all* corn but there was a lot of it there.

The flight was uneventful and a straight shot to Cincinnati, but they did have to drive another hour to reach Crown from the airport. It gave them a chance to learn about music preferences—the rental car had a top-of-the-line satellite radio option—and talk about the wedding as conversationally as possible.

She didn't expect him to memorize her great-aunt's name or which grandmother, maternal or paternal, had the cane, but it made sense if they'd been dating for a while that he'd at least know her parents' and sisters' names.

"Kelli is the oldest by six years—"

"Seven," she corrected as Gage turned left onto Pinegrove Road.

"Seven. And then comes Vanessa, Carroll, you, and Gwen is the baby."

"Very good," she praised.

Gage flashed her a smile that made her tummy tighten. He really was ridiculously good-looking. She was looking forward to showing him off.

"Mom Estelle, dad Abe, but he had to work so he's coming in the day before."

"And here I sit without my gold star stickers."

"A joke. Andrea Payne, we'll loosen you up yet."

She turned to watch out the window, her lips pressed together. Gage's hand landed lightly on her leg.

"Hey. I was kidding."

"Oh, I know." She gave him what felt like an uncomfortable smile. So much for hiding her true feelings. It seemed like he could read her mind.

"Good." He turned left and drove past the wooden fence surrounding the entrance to Crown Vineyard Resort. The resort had both a man-made lake about four miles wide as well as a vineyard on-site. It made for a beautiful backdrop in the hot summer sun, the vines draped over the hills like garlands and the water sparkling under an azure sky.

Andy had secured two suites at the resort, one next to the other. She figured she could tell everyone it was a mistake made by the front desk in case it drew attention. She couldn't very well ask Gage to stay in the same room as her. He'd already been so great about not accepting payment for being here and genuinely helping her out by remembering the main branches of her family tree.

At least that'd been her reasoning until they stood at the check-in desk at the resort and she learned that there'd been an *actual* mistake at the front desk. The suite she'd reserved for Gage, paid in full, had been given to someone else.

"Unacceptable," she said, ready to fight for what was rightfully hers.

"I'm sorry, Ms. Payne. The system must've kicked that reservation out since he wasn't on the guest list. Your reservation is still in here though," the woman said brightly. "On the ground floor, king-sized bed, and a pullout sofa if separate sleeping quarters were your main concern." The woman at the counter flashed a look from Andy to Gage, probably deciding it was terribly old-fashioned to insist on separate rooms.

Gage palmed her lower back, his hand warm, and touched his mouth to her temple. "Ground floor sounds nice," he murmured, sending droves of goose bumps down her arms. "We can have coffee on the patio in the morning, and I can always sleep on the sofa if you're uncomfortable with me in your bed."

She swallowed thickly, the visual of Gage Fleming in her bed an inviting one indeed. She shifted away from him slightly. Not because he made her uncomfortable to have him near, but because whenever he was this close she was tempted to nuzzle him like a needy cat. Physical attraction to him would be helpful to convince her family and friends at this event, but she hadn't expected it in the "off" time they had together. No one was watching them, save the inept woman who couldn't provide the additional room Andy had paid for, and yet Andy had responded to him as if she had the option to have him in her bed.

She wouldn't entertain that thought. No matter how tempting it was...

He ran his hand up her back and rested it on the back of her neck, tickling her nape with his fingers and sending chills down both of her arms.

"Honey?" He smiled down at her and she forced herself to relax. He was her boyfriend for the weekend. Might as well act like it.

"Yes. That's fine."

"Great." The woman behind the counter tapped the keys on her keyboard.

How Gage's affable mood hadn't waivered today was beyond Andy's comprehension. They'd started the morning way too early at the airport and then had gone through the discomforts of traveling—checking the bags and wedging into their tiny airplane seats. She'd fought him a little when he offered to put her bag in the overhead bin, but then realized she was standing her ground on something that shouldn't matter. If they were dating, he would of course stow her bag for her.

At the rental car kiosk, he'd insisted on driving and she'd given in on that, too. And now, the room debacle was another compromise she was making. She wasn't used to being half of a whole, or considering anyone's needs or wishes other than her own, but Gage made it easier than she'd have suspected to give up her control. It still surprised her that she'd not only let him take care of her, but that it'd also been…nice.

The woman at the front desk handed over their keycards and pointed out where their room was located, but Andy was listening with half an ear. Reason being, her mother and second eldest sister were approaching, whispering to each other as they came.

"Andrea," said Vanessa, her voice lifting in surprise.

"Hey, Ness." Andy stepped away from Gage a few inches and his hand fell away. Nervously, she smoothed her skirt with sweaty palms. "Mom."

Her mother studied Gage as well, but more dubiously than Vanessa did.

"Hi, sweetheart," her mother said, her eyes still on Gage. "Who's this?"

"Gage Fleming, this is my sister Vanessa, and my mother, Estelle."

"I've heard so much about you." Gage eased into

a grin and shook their hands, and Andy felt her spine stiffen. No way would they believe this laid-back, ridiculously handsome, socially comfortable man was dating the Ice Queen.

"When Andrea RSVP'd with a plus-one, we didn't know what to think." Her mom—a beautiful woman—managed a snide smile that was somehow still pretty.

"You're the first of your kind," Vanessa added unhelpfully. "Andrea usually shows up to her sisters' weddings by herself."

"Well, unless one of you opts to remarry," Gage said as he wrapped an arm around Andy and pulled her closer, "this will be the last one."

Oh, he was good.

"We should go find our room," Andy announced, dying to run away before she inadvertently blew their cover. She was having the hardest time being comfortable in Gage's hold, especially with her eagle-eyed family staring them down.

"You're staying together?" Estelle's voice rose along with her slim, plucked eyebrows. Not because Andy's mother was old-fashioned and believed they should be staying separately but because—

"Andrea's not known for her affection." Estelle narrowed her eyes at her daughter. Andy wanted to sink into the floor. "It's…interesting to see her as part of a…couple."

Nope, her mother did not buy that Gage was with Andy for one second. Andy felt sweat prickle under her arms and opened her mouth to share the story of how they'd met at the bar—minus the part where she offered to hire him, and adjusting the timeline some—when Gage leaned in, his lips to the shell of her ear.

"Relax, beautiful girl," he whispered. "Touch my chest and smile like I just said something deliciously dirty to you."

He hadn't said anything dirty to her but her cheeks warmed like he had. She followed his instructions, tickling her fingers over his T-shirt-covered chest and closing her eyes as she pulled her mouth into a smile. It wasn't hard to do with him so close, his low, sexy voice in her ear.

He finished by kissing her temple, and when Andy faced her mother and sister, they both looked away like the intimate public display had made them uncomfortable.

She liked that. *A lot.*

Vanessa mentioned "drinks in the bar" in an hour and then she and their mother wandered off in that direction.

Andy grinned at Gage, barely able to keep her excitement in check when she blurted, "That was amazing!"

But he wasn't smiling with her.

"Are they always that rude?"

"Who cares! You should've let me pay you. You're worth every penny."

His mouth flinched like he wanted to smile, which seemed to be his default expression. She pulled her hand off his chest, having forgotten she'd left it there this whole time. "Sorry about that."

He cupped her cheek and tipped her face up to his. She was lost, admiring his handsome face for one stunned moment. "Stop acting like we're acting. You have to immerse yourself in this role, Andy. We're always being watched."

She stole a look around the room, and sure enough, another group of family members was heading their way. "Oh. Right."

"Right. Do we need to say hi to them, too?"

"I don't feel like it."

"Okay, then, let's not." Gage lifted their bags as she shouldered her purse.

Her cousins approached, wearing matching shocked expressions, one of them going as far as to say, "Andrea. You have a date."

"One who's been itching to get her alone since this morning," Gage said. "Come on, beautiful. Let's test out that bed."

Leaving them gaping in her wake, Andy followed, wanting to punch the air in triumph. Damn, it felt good not to be alone for once. To have someone have her back—hired or no.

Maybe her fears and worries about pretending with Gage were truly unfounded. What was the harm in immersing herself in this role the same way he had?

He wasn't expecting more from her, and he'd already overdelivered on her expectations. She didn't see a reason not to return the affection Gage so easily offered. Especially when they both knew this attraction was pretend.

He walked down the long corridor toward their room and she bit her lip as she watched him carry her bags. He looked strong and sure hefting her luggage. Plus he had a great ass.

She watched his butt, satisfied that she could without worrying what anyone might say if they noticed.

Mostly pretend attraction, she thought to herself.

Seven

"My sister's husbands are nice guys for the most part," Andy was saying as she walked back and forth in the hotel room.

Ever since Gage had placed their bags on the floor in their suite, she'd been a flurry of activity from changing her clothes to touching up her makeup to fixing her hair.

"Kelli and Boyd are the snobby country-club type, but Alec, Kenny and Garrett are okay. I mean, I guess. I don't really know Garrett." She huffed as she tried again to latch a necklace around her neck and Gage stepped in to help.

"Which one's Garrett? Lift your hair." She did and he easily clasped the delicate chain at the back of her neck, smiling at a cute smattering of freckles at her nape.

"Garrett's the groom." She turned, her eyes on his, her high heels bringing them almost nose to nose. "Gwen's fiancé."

She looked away quickly, like maintaining eye contact was hard for her. When she backed away, he crooked a finger, beckoning her to him. She visibly squirmed but came as requested. Sort of.

"Closer, Andy."

One more tentative step brought her to the spot where she'd been standing a second ago.

He smoothed her hair off her neck. "You and I have been dating for eight months, right?" he asked, reminding her of their agreed-upon pretend history.

"Right."

"You're going to have to learn how to be near me without flinching. Am I that unattractive?"

"No. Not at all." She looked genuinely stricken. "I'm sorry if I made you feel that way."

He had to smile. This take-charge, in-charge woman who blew into a room like a frosty chill and froze everyone around her into submission wasn't as cold as she pretended to be.

"Andy."

"What?" Now she looked just plain hurt. "This isn't going to work, is it?"

"Yes. It's going to work." He trailed his fingers down her arm and grasped her hand, brushing her knuckles with his thumb and placing his other hand on her hip. She touched his chest like she had in the lobby, and he heard her breath hitch. "How can I make you more comfortable around me?"

"I'm not comfortable?" she seemed to ask herself. "I thought I was doing better."

So she'd been trying. Interesting.

"We should kiss," she said with a curt nod. "Get it over with."

Now he did chuckle. "Get it over with? It's not going to be like a dental appointment, Andy. I promise." He gestured to his mouth. "I know what I'm doing with this."

Her tongue darted out to wet her bottom lip as she stared at him almost in wonder. He felt the charge in the air—the sexual tension radiating between their bodies. He couldn't get past the idea that she was a live wire, even if she was contented to play the role of the "Ice Queen."

He knew this was pretend—they both did—but he couldn't help wanting to pull warm, responsive Andy from her recesses. He'd started out thinking she was a challenge, but he had the distinct impression that succeeding would be an even bigger win for her.

"I'm all for kissing you. I'll let you come to me, though. I want you to be ready. Once you touch your lips to mine, I'm going to give as good as you do," he promised. "I'll match you stroke for stroke."

"Okay." She rolled her shoulders, readying herself. "I can do this."

He banked his smile as she seemed to steel herself. She closed her eyes, pulled in a deep breath and blew it out. If he hadn't already worked with her for almost two weeks and knew what a goal-oriented achiever she was, he might've been insulted. Andy did whatever it took to win, and evidently winning included kissing him.

Her eyes popped open, determination brewing in their depths. She palmed the back of his neck and slanted her face. He leaned in, mirroring her move-ments. A fraction away from his lips, she whispered, "Are you sure you're okay with this?"

"God, yes."

As soon as he said the words, she pressed her mouth to his. It was more of a lengthy pucker than making out, but he gripped her waist to encourage her to stay close. He wanted her to take what she needed from him.

When her lips softened, he teased them open with his tongue. She slid her tongue into his mouth and that was when that live wire jolted him. She tasted like mint and smelled faintly of cinnamon. From her hair stuff or her perfume, he wasn't sure. He hadn't noticed it in the lobby, but now it infused every inch of his immediate vicinity.

He'd expected kissing Andy to affect her, and he'd expected to enjoy it. What he hadn't expected was to be towed in by her so thoroughly. The connection—the spark—that had resulted from their fusing didn't stop at their mouths.

She held onto him—her palm gripping the back of his neck, her smallish breasts against his chest—like she never wanted to let go. He tightened his hands on her hips and aligned them with his own. She was an absolutely *perfect* fit. He allowed instinct to drive him as he took the kiss deeper. What had lit between them was a hell of a lot more than he'd bargained for, but he had zero interest in stopping. Unfortunately, she did.

Andy tugged her lips from his, her delicate throat moving as she swallowed.

Gage was still leaning forward, his lips parted, completely dazed by that kiss. Here he thought he'd be the one walking her through the lesson. He'd expected to be the one guiding her. Instead, she'd taken him hostage with her mouth and her skill. He hadn't minded at all.

Take me, honey.

"So." She cleared her throat. "I guess that's not going to be a problem."

"No," he agreed with a grin. "I guess not."

"Ready to go meet the family?" She smoothed his T-shirt that she'd wrinkled in one fist while they'd kissed.

"Sure. Let's do it," he answered automatically, and then on his way down the corridor realized that the last time he'd agreed to such an invitation it'd been when Laura asked him to meet her parents.

Gage had met Andy's sisters at the bar last night—they'd been there with their husbands, who huddled together and talked like they were comfortable with each other. Rather than mingle with them, Gage had chosen to stay by Andy's side.

He was still trying to figure out the dynamic between her and her four sisters. The mother, Estelle, was stern and unfriendly, yet as gorgeous as the rest of the women. They were all tall or tallish, long-limbed and attractive, with varying shades of red or blond hair. Estelle has passed down her high cheekbones and bright blue eyes to most of her daughters.

Andy was reserved and distant, where the other sisters were mostly cozy with each other. Gage wondered if it was because she'd moved away and they'd remained in Ohio. He'd asked her as much when they returned to the room last night, but she'd only shrugged and said, "They've always been like that."

He wasn't sure if it was her sisters who'd ousted Andy or Andy who'd ousted herself. It appeared to Gage that Andy was the one keeping her distance. Although after that run-in with her mother and Ness at the front desk, who could blame her?

But Andy had come alive when Kelli asked her about work, citing her recent successes without an ounce of gravitas. Andy didn't have to overstate her accomplishments. He knew from the experience with her at Monarch—Andy was just that good.

He'd slept like crap last night since the sofa bed was about as comfortable as a pile of cotton balls and wire hangers, but he'd lied and told his pretend girlfriend that he was fine sleeping on it. She'd tried to offer him the bed and said she'd take the sofa, and then he'd had to wonder what kind of dopes she'd been dating.

Whatever ease had come as a result of the explosive kiss last night was gone by this morning. Part of him was relieved, since he'd been thrown so off-kilter by their abundant physical attraction. Andy didn't seem the type to embark on a temporary physical affair. But most of him still wanted to kiss her again and damn the consequences, if not to slake the thirst he'd developed for the confusing redhead over the last couple of weeks.

This morning's activity, according to his itinerary, was brunch with Andy's immediate family. She stalked ahead of him across the green grass, her straight spine evidence that she was back to her no-nonsense self.

The small, catered affair was for the wedding party and close family. Andy fell into both categories since she was a sister and a bridesmaid.

After a quick greeting to a few people he'd yet to meet, they lined up at the buffet packed to the edges with mini quiches, fried potatoes, fruit and every imaginable breakfast meat there was, including prosciutto-wrapped figs.

He picked up two plates and handed Andy hers.

"Thank you," she said. "I'm not accustomed to anyone fetching my plate for me."

"What cavemen have you been dating, Andy? This is boyfriend 101." Gage didn't realize anyone was paying attention to them until a bulky guy on the opposite side of the buffet table spoke.

"I was one of 'em, wasn't I, Snowflake?"

Andy bristled, her back going even straighter—Gage hadn't thought it possible. She introduced him, her voice cool and robotic. "Matthew Higgins, this is my date, Gage Fleming." Her tone softened some when she turned to Gage and said, "Matthew and I dated about seven or eight years ago."

"Oh, right. You mentioned him. The one with the protruding brow and big head." Gage kept his smile easy.

"Very funny." Matthew really did have a caveman vibe about him. He snapped his attention back to Andy. "Nice to know we regard each other with similar admiration, *Snowflake*."

"Don't call me that."

"Do you prefer Elsa?" To Gage he said, "*Frozen* wasn't out when we dated, so I had to make up my own ice-queen nickname for her."

That was what Snowflake was about?

"Freeze you out, did she?" Gage set their plates aside and pulled Andy close. His lips to her ear, he whispered, "You want a repeat of that kiss from last night, now would be a good time."

Her mouth curled into a smile of uncertainty—like maybe she thought she'd heard him wrong.

"I'm game if you are," he announced, happy to have shut out her asshole ex-boyfriend and thrilled that Andy's attention was on Gage instead. Thrilled further when Andy draped one arm over his shoulder and leaned in for a demure kiss. Not a tangle like last night, but the kiss didn't last as long as Gage would've liked.

She lowered to her heels and accepted her plate from Gage, who sent Matthew a smug smile. "She's nothing but gooey with me, big guy." He enjoyed Matthew's deep frown almost as much as him leaving pissed off.

"Thanks for that," Andy muttered as she piled her plate full of fruit. She picked through the croissants while Gage put another spoonful of scrambled eggs on his plate.

"When in doubt, make out."

Her laugh was genuine and he liked it a hell of a lot. He might have first agreed to come here in exchange for her help at Monarch, but he found he also liked protecting her from the vultures circling.

"You're not intimidated by difficult people," she pointed out. "Did you learn that at work, or is your family also challenging?"

"Sorry, can't claim dysfunction. The Flemings are scarily normal. My sister, Drew, and I are close and our parents are supportive. Although they still do weird parent stuff that embarrasses the hell out of us."

"Your sister's named Drew." Andy smiled. "What's she like?"

"She has bad taste in men, a big heart and a lot of spunk."

"Sounds like me except for the big heart. It's always been assumed that mine is missing." She sent a derisive glance in Matthew's direction.

"Sounds to me," Gage said as he placed bacon strips on his plate, "like your ex is in your head."

Eight

Andy followed beside Gage as he made his way to a table with their breakfast. He set down their plates and pulled out one of the folding chairs for her.

The theme was navy and red—Gwen's favorite colors. The tables were decorated with white tablecloths and blue vases filled with dark red roses, the silverware wrapped in navy blue cloth napkins tied with red ribbon.

Like Gwen, the décor was bold and beautiful.

Portable air conditioners stood at each corner of the tent to thwart the summer heat. Andy was glad for them since it was warm already and it was only noon.

"Care to explain your last comment at the buffet?" Gage asked as he sat across from her.

She unwrapped her silverware rather than look at him. "What?"

"Don't 'what' me. You stated you're heartless as casually as you might tell me what time it is. You can't believe that." He jerked his chin over to where Matthew sat with his girlfriend, Amber, one of Gwen's friends and bridesmaids. "You don't believe you're an ice princess."

"Ice *Queen*," she corrected, spearing a chunk of pineapple with her fork. "That was a long time ago."

"That isn't an answer."

"I know my limitations. It's part of being a good leader. I'm not warm. I can't help that."

"You were plenty warm when you kissed me a minute ago," he murmured in a low, sexy tone.

He had her there. She'd kissed him to show up Matthew, but the truth was that the second her lips touched Gage's, she'd forgotten her stupid ex was standing there. She'd been lost in Gage's mouth, in his scent. Matthew gaping unhappily was a nice bonus, though.

"That was pretending." She ate the pineapple.

"That was *not* pretending."

"Oh? Are you secretly an escort on the side?" she whispered.

"Maybe." His caramel eyes twinkled before he sent her a roguish wink. "I have been kissed enough to know the difference between a woman who's frigid and one who's—"

"Don't say out of practice." She didn't want to talk about how lame her sex life had been over the last two years. About how she'd tried to be those attributes that didn't come naturally: Bubbly, fun, laid-back. In the end the real her came forward. While she knew she wasn't heartless, she definitely kept a wall around her heart. She felt she had to after the way she'd been let down in the past. No one really understood her. No one had tried.

"I was going to say nervous." Gage's eyebrows lifted. "How long's it been?"

"Long enough that there are tumbleweeds blowing around." She didn't know what made her tell the truth. Although, maybe she did. If anyone could understand the real Andy Payne, it might be Gage. He didn't look at her like a problem to be solved. He saw her success, her timidity, her vulnerability. It'd been a while since a man had bothered to see past her cool exterior.

"Cute *and* funny." He laughed as he dug into his food and Andy was struck with the oddest sense of pride. Gage was cute and funny but she couldn't recall a single time she'd ever been accused of as much.

Throughout her childhood she'd been told she was stiff. Her mother had instructed her to "loosen up" more times than Andy could count. When she and Matthew dated, he'd asked her if she could at least "appear to be having fun" when they were out. She'd always hated that comment. Like she should smile to set everyone else at ease.

Now that she thought about it, all she did around Gage was smile. Not because he goaded her into it. He made her smile just by being himself. He made her feel comfortable even in stressful situations. He helped her crawl out of her head and be in the moment. And she'd really enjoyed kissing him in front of Matthew.

You enjoy kissing him just to kiss him...

"How long did you date that bozo, anyway?" Gage shoveled a bite of scrambled eggs into his mouth.

"A little over a year."

"A little over a year. You're going to let a guy you dated for *a little over a year*, seven or eight years ago, dictate what you think about yourself?"

"This sounds like a lecture," she pointed out blandly.

Andy was accustomed to being misunderstood and/or made to feel less-than. She could hold her own. Until she was with her family, and then those old hurts crept in and made her defensive. The difference here was that Gage was new. He was part of her work, not her personal life. She could compartmentalize that.

"Are you telling me you have no damage? That no one in your past has ever inflicted a wound that carried through into your adult years? That you didn't change some aspect of your behavior because of it?"

Gage was resolutely silent.

That was what she thought.

"Everyone has skeletons in their closets," she told him.

Before she popped a strawberry slice into her mouth, she noticed two of her sisters barreling toward her.

"Hey, you two," Gwen, the blushing bride-to-be, flicked a gaze at Gage and then back at Andy.

"Good morning, Gwen. Ready for the big day?" Gage asked. It was predictable banter but somehow it sounded fresh coming from his mouth. He really was skilled with people. Andy was better with plans. Numbers. Websites.

After Gwen answered that she was "so ready!" Andy's other sister Kelli spoke up.

"Ready for the couples' cruise today?" Kelli gave Andy a saucy wink. "It'll be Andy's first, so we're pretty excited about it."

"*Kelli*." Andy let her tone be her warning, but her eldest sister was not intimidated.

"Couples' cruise?" Gage flashed a smile at Andy and she felt her cheeks heat. She hadn't exactly called it a couples' cruise. She'd told him that they were going on a boat ride, which they were. It was a sizable pontoon boat, which was basically like a floating patio, and Andy was absolutely dreading it. Unfortunately—

"I'm making her come," Gwen chirped. "Andy is totes uncomfortable about it because she's Andy, but I want all of my sisters there."

And that was why Andy was allowing this ridiculous charade to go on. She loved Gwen, and this was her big weekend.

"It's just a boat ride," Andy told Gage, though he didn't look like he needed soothing.

"With champagne and kissing!" Gwen clapped.

"It's tradition in our family," Kelli explained, pressing her fingertips to her collarbone. "I started it with my pre-wedding festivities, and everyone has carried it forward."

"Because it's fun. All eyes will be on you two. You know what you have to do when it's your first CC."

Yep. Andy's face was flame red. She could feel it. Gage's inquisitive look paired with his indelible smile of his and then, to her sisters, he said as smooth as you please, "I look forward to finding out what that is."

What was it, exactly, that had Andy wanting to hide beneath the tablecloth right now?

Gage wasn't sure, but it intrigued the hell out of him. He bade Kelli, who had a conniving glimmer in her eye not unlike Estelle's, and Gwen adieu and turned back to his wedding date.

"Are they going to make you walk the plank or something?"

"Something like that" was the only answer he got.

After brunch Gage and Andy returned to the room to change into "boat clothes." Other than a ferry, Gage wasn't really a boat guy. Not that he was intimidated by a pontoon, or by her family. He wasn't intimidated by much, especially not the couples' cruise initiation that had made Andy twitchy since brunch.

"I packed a few towels from the room into this bag, along with…" He trailed off when Andy came out of the bedroom and into the suite, hair pulled back into a slick ponytail. She wore a gauzy white cover-up over her blue bathing suit. The sight of her legs glued his tongue to the roof of his mouth and stalled his brain. Long, pale, smooth legs. Andy was tall, and at first glance appeared almost too slim. But her curved calves and delicate ankles thwarted that notion immediately. They were subtle, but oh, yes, Andrea Payne had curves.

Her eyes rounded, and her eyebrows rose. "Along with…"

It took him a few seconds to realize he'd been in the middle of speaking.

"Sunscreen." He gestured to the bag. "You're fair-skinned, so I didn't want you to burn."

Very fair-skinned. Her freckles stood out in subtle contrast like her peachy-pink lips. Lips he'd tasted and was already itching to taste again.

"Okay, thanks." She bounced past him and he shook his head. He didn't know how, but was it possible Andy had no idea how gorgeous she was? "Ready to go?"

"Yep." Board shorts and T-shirt on, he pulled the tote over one shoulder and followed Andy to the car. Twenty minutes later they were standing on a dock in the hot summer sun while her sisters and their husbands—or fiancé in Garrett's case—settled onto the wide vinyl seats.

"Whose boat is this?" Gage asked Garrett as he settled in next to him.

"Rental. Biggest, newest one they had." Garrett was Gage's height, a few years younger, but not by much. Gage had talked to him at the bar that first night. The guy seemed cool. Kelli's husband, Boyd, waited by her side while she talked animatedly to her other sisters. Gage sensed a distinct taming-of-the-shrew feel from those two.

Vanessa's husband, Alec, took the captain's chair, wearing a captain's hat to go with it. Gage had pegged Ness as a mean girl the moment she and Estelle pecked at Andy, but he didn't think she did it on purpose. She seemed to like being in charge, though, and he could tell she approved of Alec manning the boat.

Carroll, Gage decided, was the quiet sister. She was amiable and polite, with no real dog in the fight over whether or not Andy would arrive single to the wedding. Her husband, Kenny, was as laid-back as she was, more so actually. His scraggly goatee and hippie wear gave him a definite I-smoke-weed vibe. Gage had decided Carroll and Kenny were also cool.

"Let's do this!" Gwen called, earning applause.

She was the shameless youngest child, happy with the attention, not because she craved it like Ness, but more because she expected it. Cute and plucky, she beamed with an infectious smile that was hard not to return.

Andy sat primly beside him, a pair of sunglasses on her nose and a tentative, nervous smile on her face. Gage lifted her hand in his and kept his gaze on her while he pressed his lips to her knuckles. Her smile shone as bright as the sun overhead…until Ness spoke.

"Aww! Look at those two!"

Everyone focused on them and Andy promptly stiffened and snatched her hand away.

"So shy! Honestly, Andy, who would believe you two have been dating for eight months?" Ness added and sat on Andy's immediate right on the L-shaped cushion.

"Not everyone is as comfortable making out in public as you are," Andy told her sister.

"That's true. And I happen to be really good at it," said Alec from the captain's chair.

Ness smiled, but her expression was as stiff as Andy's spine.

In moments like this, when Gage bore witness to Andy's chillier side, he felt like his past had walked over his grave. As sure as he was that Andy wasn't heartless, he had doubts that pursuing a physical relationship with her—even temporarily—was wise.

During those chillier moments, he was reminded of the idiot he'd been when he promised forever to Laura. She'd made him look like a bigger idiot when he was left holding the engagement ring she returned and the remnants of his broken heart.

Since then, Gage kept things on the surface with the women he dated. He liked women and loved sex, but getting in any deeper wasn't an option. What had started out with a simple agreement to keep Andy on board at Monarch had turned into meeting her complex family, and her ham-handed ex-boyfriend.

And yet he couldn't help coming to Andy's rescue and changing the subject.

"I notice Estelle didn't make the trip," he said to Ness.

"This is a sibling-only affair." Ness swept her hair off her neck and piled it on top of her head in a sloppy bun.

"Hang on to something," Alec announced as they puttered from the no-wake zone into the larger portion of the lake. Cheered on by his passengers, he pushed the speedometer to the middle, sending Andy's ponytail whipping behind her.

Gage settled back, his arm on the bench and Andy sent him what appeared to be a gracious smile. She leaned back into the curve of his arm and he rested his palm on her shoulder. Whatever cooler moments he'd witnessed from her, she was warm where it counted. Andy was completely responsive to him and he enjoyed the hell out of getting her to respond.

Enough lingering in the past. He'd rather sit here, his arm around Andy, and enjoy the cool breeze, hot sun and random splashes of water kicked up by the buoys on the sides of the boat.

Nine

Alec dropped anchor in a private cove surrounded by trees and a few villas. Kelli and Ness opened coolers and divvied out drinks into plastic flutes. Sparkling rosé for the ladies, and ales brewed and canned by a local brewery for the guys.

Andy gladly accepted her drink, letting the bubbles tickle her throat and relying on the summer sun as well as the alcohol to take her down a notch.

Or ten.

No one made her as prickly as her sisters. She wasn't like them—any of them. Sure she might have a dose of Kelli's self-assuredness, but Andy didn't have her eldest sister's confident, sexy vibe. And while Ness was a go-getter, she wasn't plagued by Andy's shyness. Carroll was genuine and sweet, whereas Andy had never been referred to as "sweet," and the bride-to-be, Gwen, was adorable and fun. Andy hadn't been accused of being either of those.

She was the black sheep among her reddish-flaxen-haired sisters, sharing their coloring but not their personalities. Every time she was around them she felt as if there was an invisible yardstick measuring her to see if she'd blossomed into a *Payne lady* yet, and if her mother's assessment was anything to go by—Andy hadn't.

She'd settled for being the best at her job, and excelling in her field rather than competing socially. They all knew what she did for a living—that she was the mysterious Andy Payne who was often imitated, never duplicated—but praise was more often given for personality and looks—especially by her former-beauty-queen mother.

As a teen Andy had been lanky, thinner than any of her sisters. Fairer, too. By age sixteen her nose was a touch long and her feet a *not*-dainty size ten, and she'd felt firmly entrenched into the black-sheep role she'd assigned herself.

She'd moved away from Crown, Ohio, to become someone else, someone new. Someone who wouldn't be contrasted and compared to her sisters. Her nose was still a touch too long, she was as curve-free as she ever was, and her feet were still a size ten, but she'd used her frosty personality to help build an empire. And she wasn't as socially awkward as she used to be. She was open and polite, even if she didn't exude warmth.

"That went fast," Gage said, taking her empty plastic flute. "Can I refill it for you?"

"Yes."

He pushed his sunglasses on top of his head and studied her, his eyes a lighter shade of brown in the sunlight. The stubble on his chin and jaw was short and rakish, his hair windblown and curling on the ends.

"You have nice hair."

The moment the words were out of her mouth she wanted to die. What a boring compliment. Not to mention it was more the kind of thing you'd say to someone when you'd just met them, not after you'd been in a relationship for eight months. Thankfully no one was paying attention to them or she would've just given away that they'd known each other only a few weeks. Her brothers-in-law were behind them stripping off their shirts to dive in and her sisters were huddled over the ice-filled coolers at the front of the boat, chatting.

"So do you." He wrapped her long ponytail around his fist and gave it a subtle yank, smiling as easy as you please. She swallowed thickly, unsure what to do with the attention.

"H-has it always been curly?" she stammered. Gage looked at her with a combination of heat and admiration, curiosity and a bit of bemusement. Like she was a puzzle he wanted to solve. Another new feeling for her. "Sorry. Stupid question. Of course it's always been curly."

"The bane of my existence." His smile didn't budge. "I try to keep it short, but it still curls." He pushed his hand through his hair again and the wave snapped right back into place. She had to grin. And before she thought of what she was doing, her hand was in his hair, sweeping the strands. It was soft and thick, adding a boyish charm to a man who was *all* man.

"You two are positively adorable," Gwen said, sneaking up on them. Although, you couldn't really "sneak" on a twenty-four-foot boat. Andy had been completely absorbed in her pretend boyfriend. "Did you pick your movie yet?"

"Movie?" Gage asked as Andy returned her hands to her lap.

Gwen aimed her wide grin at Andy. "You didn't tell him." Back to Gage, she said, "If it's your first couples' cruise as a couple, you have to reenact a movie kiss for everyone. Extra points for authenticity."

"Boyd and I did *Gone with the Wind*," Kelli announced proudly. "Ness, *Dirty Dancing*—"

"Complete with dance moves," Vanessa called over.

"And Carroll," Gwen said, "chose *The Princess Bride*, while I went with *Twilight*." The youngest of the Payne sisters swooned. "How I love my sparkly vampires."

"Sorry I missed that one," Andy said, genuinely meaning it. She hadn't made it home for the engagement party here at the resort, which is when the *Twilight* magic must've occurred.

"It's your turn now," Carroll told Andy. "Don't screw it up."

"But first, swimming! It's too hot not to jump in." Gwen tore off her cover-up and revealed a perfect-ten body complete with a belly-button piercing she'd insisted was still "in." A tattoo graced her shoulder blade, a smattering of butterflies and flowers in full color. When her groom called down for her to jump, she did.

Kelli wrinkled her nose. "I'm not getting in that water."

Vanessa agreed and they moved to the other end of the boat farthest from Andy and Gage, while Carroll argued they were "spoilsports" and leaped in behind Gwen.

"Movie kiss, huh?" Gage asked.

"The good ones are already taken," Andy argued.

"Not true. There are lots of great movie kisses available. What about *Dumb and Dumber*, where he tries to eat her face?" At Andy's aghast expression, he chuckled. "I'm kidding."

"I was thinking more like *Lady and the Tramp*. What could we use as spaghetti?" She looked around at a few ropes and wrinkled her nose. Definitely not. But something similar—something tame and not embarrassing.

"What about *The Notebook*?" he asked. "The kiss in the rain is iconic."

It was also…intimate. Plus, Gage would have to lift her and that would be weird. It wasn't as if Andy was dainty.

"No," she told him. "It's not raining."

He narrowed his eyelids as if he knew why she'd bowed out of that suggestion. Then his face lit up. "I've got it."

"What?"

"Nah, I'm not letting you shoot this one down or reason us out of it. I'll tell you right before it happens."

"What if I haven't seen the movie?"

"Trust me. You have."

"What if I haven't?" She liked being prepared—especially for a kiss in front of her relatives.

"You have. But if you haven't, I'll walk you through it."

But that didn't make her feel any better. Her stomach jumped in anticipation, nervousness and excitement switching places in a do-si-do.

"Why me?"

She blinked at the question. "Sorry?"

"Why did you approach me in the bar that night and offer to pay me two grand?" he asked, his voice low so as to not be overheard. "Were you out of options, or was there something else?"

She studied his rakish curls, warm caramel irises and affable smile. She could lie, but she decided not to. "You looked nice."

She winced, worrying that the comment was almost a repeat of the "nice hair" one earlier, but Gage grinned.

"And? Am I?"

"Very."

There was a distinct pause where they watched each other and the pretending seemed to fall away. A moment where Andy caught a glimpse of the possibility of more if she would only open herself up to it… if only he would.

She blinked to break the intense eye contact and Gage's smile snapped seamlessly into place.

"Take this off and swim with me." He plucked the edge of her cover-up.

"That's okay."

"No. It's not. It's a hundred-and-fifty degrees out here. Let's get wet."

Something about the way his voice dropped suggestively made her consider doing more than kissing him. If her tingling innards were anything to go by, she was starting to consider a host of other possibilities.

Naughty possibilities.

"Your face is red already. See? You're hot." He tugged at her cover-up and she let him take it off, holding her arms overhead. She was hot, all right. When the white gauzy material was done obstructing her vision, she came face-to-face with an expression on Gage she'd never seen before. Playful was his typical MO, but this look was…fiery.

Heated and scintillating.

Suggestive, and not in the "pretend" way.

"Hot," he repeated, his smirk twitching his lips. "Damn, Andy." He took her hand and helped her to her feet. Then he grabbed the personalized tote that read Gwen ♥ Garrett where he'd stuffed their towels and sunscreen and produced a bottle.

Wide, warm hands on her hips, he turned her. "I'll do your back."

Gage momentarily lost the thread of whatever he was talking about when he removed Andy's cover-up.

Beneath the shapeless square material was hiding a lithe body. Her shoulders were delicate and round, freckles dotting them like they'd been misted on with a spray bottle. Her back was muscular and strong, and he noticed more freckles as he smoothed sunscreen over her shoulders. There was something intimate about slipping his fingers under the straps of her suit, especially where her bikini top tied into a bow at the middle of her back. His fingers flinched as he imagined tugging that string loose and releasing her breasts, maybe smoothing his hands around to cup them. He'd thought she was a B-cup, but now that she was mostly undressed, he guessed she bordered on a C.

Leaning close to her ear, he said, "Is this okay?"

"Hmm?" She sounded distracted, like maybe she'd been enjoying his hands on her skin as much as he was.

"Are you comfortable with my touch?" He applied the cream to her lower back and braced her sides with his hands. "This is how our kiss will happen," he murmured into her right ear. "I want to make sure I'm not weirding you out."

In a perfect reenactment of what was to come, she turned over her shoulder to look at him, blue eyes wide and curious. A high-pitched voice rang out—Gwen's.

"They're doing it! I know the movie!" she called up from the water.

Gage jerked his attention to the guys and girls in the water, and then to Kelli and Ness on the boat. Everyone was watching.

"No practicing! Do it now!" Gwen shouted with a happy laugh.

"Gage?" Andy's voice was a soft, curious pant. "What are we doing?"

He slid his hands up her waist, lifting her arms

and holding them straight out to her sides. He walked her forward to the edge of the boat as their audience cheered.

"*Titanic*!" Carroll shouted.

Over her shoulder, Andy sent him a smile.

"You've seen it?" he asked.

"Of course."

"Then you know what comes next." He tugged her hair from her ponytail, releasing the silken strawberry blond strands, gripped her waist and lingered over her shoulder. As if God was helping out, a breeze kicked her hair at same moment she turned her face to his and he lowered his lips.

The kiss was soft and expected, but what was unexpected was the way her curved bottom nestled perfectly against his crotch as he used every faculty in his brain to keep from hardening against her. She raised a hand to the back of his neck in perfect movie form and held him against her, her fingernails tickling into his hair as he moved his lips over hers.

More cheering erupted from the water and on the boat and Andy eased away from him. Perfectly comfortable and confident.

He loved seeing her that way around her family. Since they'd arrived, she'd been walking on eggshells…or thumbtacks, depending on which of her family members was around. Now, though, the feisty glimmer in her eyes was one he'd seen time and time again in a business setting, where she was cocksure and definitive.

Nothing turned him on more. Especially when she reacted that way to him.

"I'm calling it, guys," Gwen shouted. "Best couples' cruise kiss. Now you two have to stay together forever. You just won first place."

Ten

Andy showered after Gage, insisting he go first so she could take her time. He agreed since his showers took all of two minutes. Now he sat on their suite's sofa, where he was watching TV. The true crime documentary wasn't keeping him from picturing her in there, water sluicing down her trim form and droplets hanging off nipples he'd seen the outline of in her bikini top but had yet to taste.

"Dammit." He adjusted a budding erection and addressed his lap. "We're faking. Understand?"

That wasn't sinking in for any part of his anatomy, including his brain. After the *Titanic* kiss, they'd swum in the lake, the water warm on the surface and bone-chillingly cold at their feet. Since it was sand-bottomed, they'd found water about four feet deep to stand in while everyone enjoyed beer or rosé and the coolness of the water in contrast to the baking-hot sun.

During that time, Gage allowed himself to touch Andy freely and she'd glided against him, her skin slippery from the combo of smooth water and creamy sunscreen, turning him on in a way he hadn't known possible.

She was his colleague, and this was an act. She'd made that clear when she'd invited him, and by footing the bill for his stay. But he couldn't escape the niggling feeling that she was enjoying herself as much as he was. That their chemistry was hot enough that her sisters kept pointing it out.

She'd thwarted her sisters' teasing by batting her lashes at Carroll and rolling her eyes at Ness, but Andy liked him. He could tell. She responded to him. If they were to go to bed together, he would blow her mind.

The only problem was that he wasn't confident he could disentangle from her as easily as he had from, say, Heather, the last woman he'd dated. What he'd experienced with Andy so far—whether working closely with her at Monarch, or hanging out with her family—was deeper than mere surface attraction. Sex wouldn't dampen the simmering attraction between them. It would *ignite* it.

That would make walking away harder and Gage would eventually have to walk away.

The bathroom door swung aside, steam billowing from the small space. Andy emerged, her cheeks rosy, her hair wet and combed straight, a white towel wrapped around her body.

Speaking of igniting...

"I'm sunburned." She pouted.

"What? How?" He moved to her, flicking the TV off as he went and tossing the remote onto the couch.

"I don't know. Maybe the sunscreen washed off."

She turned around and peeked over her shoulder, reminding him of the boat kiss and the press of her ass against his front. He swallowed a groan.

"Here." She pressed two fingers into her red shoulder and the color changed to creamy pale before quickly fading to red again.

"Does it hurt?" He repeated the move on her back where her reddened skin resembled her shoulders. "Did the hot water of the shower hurt?"

She paused in thought. "No. Not really."

"Then you're fine." He smoothed his fingers along her back and over her shoulder, the feel of her soft skin having a drugging effect on him. Touching her sent his fears of future entanglements up in smoke. The devil on his shoulder assured him she'd be worth it, and damned if the angel on his other shoulder didn't agree.

She came closer and gazed up at him with an earnest gaze almost as naked as she was. Such vulnerability.

Those warning bells made one more attempt to stop him but he justified that Laura had never had this much vulnerability in her eyes.

Or was that longing?

Only one way to find out.

"Do you have any idea how sexy you are?" he murmured.

Her reaction wasn't a gasp of surprise or a sigh of capitulation but instead a challenging smile followed by "Ha! You must have me confused with Gwen. Or Kelli. Or…any of my sisters."

She threw a hand of dismissal that he caught in midair. He tugged her to him, and she gripped her towel with one hand to keep it from slipping.

More's the pity.

"No. I mean you." He didn't smile, making sure she knew he wasn't playing around. "You're sexier than all your sisters put together."

"Gage." She released her hand and patted his chest as if leveling with him. "Save this stuff for an audience."

He gripped her waist and pulled her against him, her towel gaping when she let it go to steady herself by grabbing his biceps.

She didn't believe him.

She had no idea how sexy she was. And that invited a fun challenge that far outweighed his concerns of getting in too deep.

"Want me to show you?" He had to ask. She was too skittish to ask him for what she needed. Plus, he respected her. If she had no desire to find out what he had in mind for her tonight, he'd go back to that horrible pullout sofa bed. He'd go there rock-hard and in need of an ice bath, but he'd survive.

"Show me what?"

He stroked his fingers over her collarbone to her shoulder. "Well. I could point out that you're delicate and strong at the same time." He gripped the towel hanging precariously on her body, holding it closed but allowing his fingers to graze her cleavage. "Then I could mention how much I'm dying to see your breasts after they teased me by bobbing in the lake in that sexy string bikini top you wore."

Her smile slid away, lust blowing out her pupils.

"My breasts...?" Her brow crimped like that phrase didn't compute.

"And those legs." He closed his eyes, flared his nostrils and grunted for effect. "They've been killing me since you started working at Monarch."

"Gage..."

"Am I making you uncomfortable?" His eyes moved to her pink mouth.

"No. I—I was going to ask you if you were serious about showing me."

Hard-on. *Achieved*. His shorts tented and he shifted to bump into her hip.

"Hell, yes, I'll show you. Over and over if you like." He grinned. Excited. Wanting that.

"No making fun of me." She pointed, her voice stern, her finger an inch away from his face. He bit it and soothed the bite by suckling and then letting go in a long, smooth motion.

She licked her lips in anticipation.

"Definitely, you're in need of a lesson, Andy. That is...if this is a yes." He had to be crystal clear she wanted this.

"Yes," she breathed.

Oh, it was *on*.

He yanked her towel aside and dropped it in a damp pile at her feet.

Cool, air-conditioned air hit her body as goose bumps rose on her arms. Gage kept his hands on her sides, but the look in his eyes was feral in the best way. He wanted *her*. He thought she was sexier than all her sisters combined.

She dismissed the possibility that he'd lied about how attractive he found her simply to get into her pants—or *towel* as it were. Andy was no dummy. She'd worked with Gage in close proximity and had been around him enough to see his guard dropped. Gage might very well be the last salesman on the planet who wasn't full of crap.

Which meant he'd been sincere about every nice thing he'd said to her.

"I want to look so bad," he said with an impish smile, and then she realized he meant down at her nude body. He'd kept those melted-caramel eyes on hers ever since he pulled her towel off. The fact that she still held his gaze was a powerful feeling indeed.

Confidence surged through her at earning his attention, at holding the cards. Her *yes* determined how far they went tonight. He'd made that abundantly clear.

Hands on his T-shirt, she gripped twin fists of the material and tugged upward. "I'll show you mine if you show me yours."

"Deal." He had the shirt off in record time and she thanked the good Lord for her sight. Gage's chest was beautiful. The strong, firm pectoral muscles and ridges of his abs. He wasn't so much thick as lean, his waist tapering to a tantalizing V that disappeared into his shorts. Shorts that were straining against a part of him that was definitely, if outer appearances were to be believed, *thick*.

She lifted her eyes to apologize for ogling, only to find his gaze on the ceiling.

"Gage," she whispered, leaning in and brushing her lips over his. There was a benefit to being almost as tall as he was, though now that she was sans heels, she had to climb to her toes a little. "You can look now."

He cocked an eyebrow and lowered his eyes, his smile fading into an expression of awe as he perused her body. He took a full step back, holding her hands out at her sides.

"Damn."

Were a headshake and a *damn* signs of disappointment? She wasn't sure…

"Not what you expected?" She tittered a nervous laugh.

"No." He didn't let her squirm away, cupping a breast and thumbing her nipple. "Better."

His other hand held her jaw and he didn't wait for her to answer before he kissed her, sliding his tongue into her mouth to tangle with hers.

They made out long and slow, his hand moving from one breast to the other as her tender buds peaked at the attention. Her wet hair dripped down her back, leaving trails of water over her backside and doing a good job of mimicking the wetness between her legs.

By the time Gage moved to her neck and was tonguing the very sensitive patch of skin behind her ear, she was wrestling with his shorts and shoving them down his thighs.

"There she is." He sent her a grin that could only be described as wicked. "I've been waiting for you to let go with me, Andy. Since you stalked over to me in that bar, I knew this was in there. All that cool control didn't fool me for a second. You take what you want, don't you, sweetheart?"

Her heart thudded like it'd punched the air in triumph.

She *did* take what she wanted.

At work. In her business life.

But in her personal life, she'd never been so bold.

It was Gage.

He provided a very big safety net for her high-wire routine. Maybe it was their arrangement, or maybe it was simply him. He was easy to be around, comfortable in his own skin, and she'd begun replicating his smooth confidence.

"Are you asking me to take you?" she asked, her smile incurable.

"No. I'm *telling* you to take me. Have at it." He held his arms to his sides as his shorts slid past his knees. Somehow, with his shorts around his ankles and his boxers distorted by the ridge of his erection, he didn't look silly. He looked *scrumptious*.

"We're doing this." She freed him and shoved his boxers down, stomping on them with her bare feet.

He stepped from the inconvenient clothing and kissed her again, moving them to the couch. "Wait, not there. I've slept on floors that are more comfortable."

He routed them through the living room to the tiny kitchenette instead, which wasn't all that far away given the diminutive size of the suite.

"Why didn't you tell me?" Concern wrinkled her forehead. "I would've let you have the bed."

"I know." He gripped her waist and plopped her onto the tiny square of countertop. He had to move the mini coffeepot aside and bodily brace her against the counter to keep her from toppling off.

"What are you doing?" she asked through a laugh.

A laugh! While she was naked, damp parts of her freshly showered body sticking to his sexy, tanned form... She'd never had sex and laughed at the same time. What was it about this guy?

"Countertop sex. I hope. We have a serious real estate problem." He looked behind them at the tiny table and chairs that might collapse under the weight of a stern glance. "Not many options around here."

"What about the bed?"

"*Definitely* the bed. I was saving that for tonight." He kissed her softly. "Assuming I impress you enough to earn a repeat."

"Hate to break it to you..." Looping her arms around his neck, she rested her forearms on his trapezoids and tilted her head. "But considering how long it's been for me, and how forgettable sex has been in my recent and not-so-recent past, that bar is pretty low."

Eleven

And she's funny.

Funny in a clever way. He found nothing funny about her admitting she'd had forgettable or bad sex in the past. He found it…exhilarating. Not to brag—what the hell, it wasn't bragging if it was true, right?—but Gage didn't leave women unsatisfied. And he was never forgettable. Which was part of the problem, since the women he slept with began nudging him toward boyfriend status pretty soon after they did the deed.

He wanted to have a release with Andy—to experience every amazing part of her lithe body—but he also wanted to show this woman how beautiful she was. It seemed like no one had taken the time or effort to show her, and that was a crime.

She didn't curl away from him or appear the least bit bashful now. If she'd been honest about the mediocre sex in her past, he'd raise the bar so fucking high no one would ever compete with him. Gage aimed for 100 percent success in all attempts and right now, with a wet and willing Andy Payne holding onto him and smiling at him like he was her shiny new present, he'd happily blow her mind.

"Ever done it on a hotel countertop?"

"Can't say that I have." She wobbled and he steadied her by pressing against her. The move had the added effect of his hard-on rubbing against her slick folds and, *God have mercy*, did she feel warm and welcome and good.

So good.

"I have a condom in my purse," she told him, then offered a chagrined twist of her mouth. "It's really old, though."

"Mine aren't." He didn't miss the subtle flinch. He cradled her face with one palm. "I don't mean because I had sex recently. I meant because I *bought* them recently."

"When is the last time you had sex?"

"Long enough."

"I'll tell you how long it's been for me."

"Andrea."

"Yes?"

"Do you want to talk or do you want to fuck?"

He tested her with the harsh word to learn what she liked. To his delight a smile burst forth on her face. "The second one."

Then she bit her lip and his erection gave a happy jerk.

"Okay, then. Don't fall off this countertop while I grab a condom from my bag."

"Okay." She kicked her legs back and forth, knocking the cabinets with her heels and sending her breasts bouncing in a rhythm he could watch all day. He raced back to her, fumbling with the packet, and she took it from his hand.

"Gage Fleming, I think you must be excited." Package ripped open, she reached for him. "Do you mind?"

"From now on, you don't have to ask that." He held the back of her neck as she rolled the condom on. He watched her long, graceful fingers as she sheathed him, and let out a groan.

"Did you like that?" she asked.

"I like everything you do to me. Haven't you figured that out yet?" At her entrance, he nudged, his gaze drilling into hers. He notched the head, blew out a breath and closed his eyes. Nerves tingled and his arms shook. He hadn't been this excited to slide home in...*a while*. More than that, he hadn't been this intrigued by the prospect of sex since he was a hell of a lot younger.

"Gage, yes." She sighed, a breathy exhale that tore him open. He obeyed her tugging hands and slipped inside of her, slowly thrusting as her eyelids sank to half-mast and her mouth dropped open in ecstasy.

This. This was *fantastic*.

"You feel so good," she breathed, wrapping her ankles around his butt to pull him forward on the next long slide.

She raked her nails into his hair and he slammed his mouth over hers.

"So thick," she gasped when their mouths parted. "Big. No. *Huge*."

He gave her a pleading look. "Andy. Keep that up and this will end a lot sooner than you want it to. Got it?"

She bit her lip and nodded and that sweet, chaste expression did absolutely nothing to help him pull himself together.

He'd started this physical interaction to show her how sexy she was and yet she'd turned the tables, flattering him so much he could hardly keep his head in the game.

Scooping her to him, he tilted her hips and sank into her again. She let out a squeak of delight, her nails scraping his back.

"Yesss," she hissed in his ear. She only got louder as he continued working them into a sweaty lather, especially when he found her G-spot and pulled her down on him hard. It was awkward and clumsy at first but now she clung to him, her limbs wrapped around his while she finished him off. When she shouted her release, he buried his face in her neck and let go.

Seconds, minutes or, hell, hours, he didn't know, later, he surfaced from her cinnamon-scented skin to give her a lazy smile. It was one Andy returned, her cheeks rosy, her body sated and lazily draped over his as he held them against the countertop with what little strength he had left.

"How was that?" he asked, shameless.

The sex had been incredible and he was fishing for as many compliments as she'd dole out.

Fingers finding the curls of his hair, her mouth widened in an equally shameless grin. "You've proven you know your way around a countertop. I guess we'll see what you can do tonight in bed."

* * *

The wine tasting that evening doubled as a bachelorette/bachelor party for the bride and groom. Since this was a private event, the wedding party plus guests had the run of the patio, which had been decorated with strings of twinkle lights.

Andy was impressed by how low-key Gwen had kept the weekend's festivities. Her itinerary was nothing like Kelli's or Ness's had been—which were almost military standard by their punctual schedules—though Andy was sure if she was a bride in the future, she'd be much less laid-back than Gwen or Carroll. Gwen's wedding was happening at breakneck speed, somehow fitting in brunch, boating and a wine tasting along with a bachelor/bachelorette party into a single Friday.

"This is such a beautiful venue. Were all of you married here?" Amber, Gwen's good friend and Matthew's date, asked. Andy's ex-boyfriend wasn't sitting with the girls but with the guys, who'd poured cognac instead of wine and held unlit cigars on the other side of the winery's huge patio.

"I started it," Kelli announced, her I'm-the-first-born-and-pioneer-of-all attitude shining through. "I found the venue and Boyd agreed it'd be perfect. Vanessa followed suit."

"Only because they had the option to be married in the vineyard," Ness defended.

"It's so funny that you all married in order, too!" Amber exclaimed with a sweep of her hand. When that hand reached Andy, Amber caught her mistake. "Oh, well. Almost in order."

Andy gave the other woman a brittle smile. *Rub it in.*

"I'm sure Andy will choose a venue that is on the West Coast when she weds," Ness said. "She's always been one to do her own thing and snub tradition."

Kelli sent a smirk to Andy that wasn't hard to decode. *If she gets married.*

"I'd love to see what kind of beautiful West Coast wedding you come up with, Andy. I bet it'd be gorgeous." Carroll smiled in support and Andy appreciated her sister speaking up for her.

"How long have you and Gage been seeing each other?" This from Amber.

"Eight months," Andy answered automatically.

"So, it's serious," Amber said.

"Looked pretty serious on the boat this afternoon." Kelli trilled.

"Yeah, I thought maybe he'd come as a friend until I saw that kiss," Ness said. "Not to mention you are absolutely glowing-happy right now."

Andy blinked around. The girls were sitting in a circle on metal chairs around a firepit dotted with citronella candles. They were all nodding their agreement.

"What happened after the boat and before this wine tasting, anyway?" Carroll asked with a teasing wink as she raised her wineglass to her lips.

A rush of confidence pushed a smile to Andy's lips. "Oh, you know. We went back to the room and showered. Then…watched some TV," she said coyly.

A round of *woots* and giggles lifted on the air and she looked up in time to see Gage smiling his approval.

She wasn't used to taking her sisters' teasing in stride, but their playful pokes didn't so much as ruffle a single one of Andy's feathers. She supposed she had Gage to thank for that, too. He'd praised her for being sexy, had turned her on like a light switch and then made love to her standing up, giving her the discretion to invite him to her bed tonight.

Andy had practically floated here on a balloon filled with her own confidence. Confidence at work, she was used to. Confidence around her family was a whole other experience.

One she embraced.

"You two are seriously compatible," Gwen said, noticing Andy and Gage's eye-lock from across the patio. "I love you together. Reminds me of me and Garrett when we first met."

"Which was what, about seven minutes ago?" Ness teased, and everyone laughed.

Gwen and Garrett had been seeing each other less than two months when Gwen announced her engagement. As crazy as it'd been to receive that email from her sister, Andy had passed it off as kismet. True love had the reputation of finding people when they weren't looking for it.

Andy bit her lip in thought. True love wasn't what was between her and Gage, but there seemed to be *something* there. She wasn't willing to deny herself the experience of sex with him, but now that it'd happened she wondered what life would be like when they returned to Seattle. When she followed up with him to ask how the team was doing in the office. She'd only asked for his help for the weekend…but what if it blossomed into more?

Did she want it to?

"Gage is yummy. Am I allowed to say that?"

Carroll refilled her wine and gave Andy a cute but slightly sloppy wink.

"Yes. I think we can all drink to that. If it's not too weird for Andy that we objectify her date," Ness said.

"Gage can handle it." Andy sneaked a glance to find him laughing with the guys, though when he ducked his head to take a drink from his glass, she noted him glaring at Matthew. That made her like him more.

"Those curls are to die for. He has this sort of schoolboy charm," Kelli said. "But one look at his ass and it's clear he's all man."

Andy blushed, but couldn't help adding, "You should see the rest of him."

Howls of laughter erupted in their circle and Gwen gripped Andy's forearm in support. "I love you like this! So open and happy. It's awesome."

It *was* awesome. Andy shook her head, but not in disagreement—in surprise. "I guess I always felt like the black sheep. The odd one out."

Gwen abruptly sobered, her eyebrows twin slashes of concern. "We don't see you that way."

"At all," Kelli chimed in.

"If anything you're the pioneer of all of us," Carroll agreed. "Over there in the big city making a name for yourself."

"Living life on your own terms," Ness added, and Andy blinked at her in shock.

Whatever brought forth that moment of rallying, whether the wine or the weather, Andy welcomed it.

"Thanks, guys." She raised her wineglass. "Cheers to Gwen and Garrett!"

Everyone joined in on the toast and Andy, as relieved as she was to have the attention off her, also allowed a little part of her to bask in the newfound feeling of fitting in.

Twelve

Gage caught Andy peering over her wineglass at him and had to smile. Damn, but his sexy strawberry-haired vixen would be the death of him. And if that was the way he'd go, he was sure he'd die a happy man.

Nothing had turned him on more than turning her on. Watching as she surprised herself by liking him so much, by liking sex on the countertop so much. He'd enjoyed the delighted, satisfied smile on her face as much as he'd enjoyed the sex itself. Pleasing her pleased him, and the prospect of doing it with her in a bed tonight was a welcome one. Especially after she'd had a few glasses of wine and was loose and sleepy.

Whatever flashbacks of his ex-fiancée had haunted him before, he was glad to have pushed them aside in favor of indulging with Andy.

"You and Andy, huh?" Matthew Higgins, known to the rest of the guys as "Higgs," asked.

It was rhetorical, though, a way to bring up Andy and goad Gage into a fight. Gage knew Matthew's type. Mean. Stupid. The kind of guy who had to prove he was the biggest, strongest man in any gathering. Gage couldn't care less about bravado. He knew exactly what Matthew's insistence on drawing attention to himself meant. It meant that Matthew had a small dick.

"She's always been a puzzle," said Kenny, who stroked his beard in thought. "But then I saw you two together and it was like the puzzle was a whole picture."

"Uh, thanks." But Gage's smile, though slightly perplexed, was also grateful. Ness's husband, Alec, spoke next.

"Andy surprised us, is what Kenny means, I think." Kenny gave him a thumbs-up, and Alec's eyebrows jumped. "Anyway. She's been a loner for as long as I've known her. Except, well…when she dated him." He gestured to Matthew, who puffed out his chest.

Moron.

"Eh, Andy and I weren't long for this world. She doesn't mesh with me. She's brisk and curt. Professional and cold. Smart as a whip, though. I'll give her that."

Gage's blood was set to simmer. Between clenched teeth, he managed, "Must've been you."

Matthew's lips oozed into a smile. "That so? Did you thaw our little Ice Queen, Gage?"

"She's not *our* anything, prick." Gage's anger spiked and he took a step toward the larger, dumber man. Andy might not belong to Gage, either, but he'd be damned if he'd let her ex stake some sort of claim over her.

"Okay, Higgs." Alec put a hand on Gage's chest and patted a few times. "Last thing Gwen and Garrett need is a fistfight on their wedding weekend."

"If you do anything to make Gwen cry, I'll beat your ass myself," Garrett promised, his eyes on Matthew. "Including upsetting her best friend, your date."

Garrett capped off that statement with a smile, but it was a humorless one.

"Far be it from me to ruin anyone's weekend," Matthew grunted. To Gage, he said, "If Andy's happy with you, I guess congratulations."

"Gee, thanks, Higgs," Gage grumbled.

"I like Andy," Garrett told him, trimming the end of his cigar and passing the trimmer to Gage. "She's probably like the rest of our girls in that there's another layer to her when you two are alone. Another side of her that she doesn't share with the world."

"Gwen has a side other than bubbly and cute?" Alec asked, disbelieving. "And here I thought she was a fairy princess."

The rest of the guys chatted about their wives, but Gage found his mind wandering to his own Payne royalty. Gwen was a fairy princess, and Andy believed she was the Ice Queen—no thanks to the Neanderthal "Higgs" across from him who puffed on his cigar. Matthew had set himself away from the guys as if by choice, but they'd shunned him by subtly turning their backs.

Gage peeked over at Andy, who was sitting, legs crossed, in a pair of white capri pants and a radiant red blouse. She was smiling, her wineglass aloft, her eyes light and happy. It was so good to see her comfortable around the women she'd compared herself to for years and never thought she'd measure up to.

Gage had told Andy she was sexier than all of her sisters combined and he'd meant it. He perused the Payne women, including her mother, who was just joining them, and noticed a tall, older man—Andy's father, Gage would bet—angling for the guys.

Andy stood out in stark contrast from the women surrounding her because he knew that secret side of her the guys had hinted their wives had, too. Gage knew a part of Andy few others did, and that made him want to uncover more.

"Well, well. If it isn't the man who's stealing away my baby girl." The tall man with white hair boomed as he held out a hand to Garrett.

"Abe. Good to see you." Garrett straightened some, taking the man's hand in a solid pump.

Greetings happened all around, with newcomer Garrett visibly less comfortable around Abe Payne than the rest of the guys. Admittedly Gage also felt a pinch of discomfort when Abe settled his navy eyes on him.

"You must be Andrea's date."

"Gage Fleming." He shook Abe's wide palm, noting the way Andy's father hulked over him, and Gage wasn't a short guy.

"Hmm. Surprised she brought someone."

Gage prepared for a comment like Estelle's or Vanessa's had about Andy not being able to scrounge up a date, but Abe surprised him by saying, "She's usually too independent and discerning to bring a date. Except for this bozo." He shot a thumb over his shoulder at Matthew, who for once looked nervous.

"How are you, sir?" Matthew extended a hand. A hand Abe ignored before sending a barely tolerant headshake to Gage.

Gage grabbed a cigar from the table behind him. "Cigar?" he offered Abe, suddenly a big fan of Andy's father.

"Thank you, Gage." Abe clapped his shoulder. "I think we're going to get along just fine."

"One more, c'mon!" Gwen goaded as she tipped the bottle of chardonnay precariously over Andy's glass. It was the end of the last bottle, however many that'd been. The waitress had efficiently removed the empties, which made counting hard.

"*Fine.* But that's it," Andy acquiesced as Gwen drained the last few ounces of wine from the bottle to the glass.

The Payne women, with their Irish blood, were no strangers to *the drink*. Andy's mother, Estelle, sat rosy-cheeked and laughing, her air of superiority drowned after the first glass. Kelli and Vanessa had relaxed, too, and Carroll and Gwen were punchy and giggly…even more so than usual.

Andy was somewhere in between, as she'd always been with her sisters. She wasn't as ruthlessly serious as her older sisters, but not as laid-back as the other two. She'd often landed in the middle, and where they'd been comfortably paired off with each other, she supposed it made sense why she'd labeled herself the odd woman out.

"Oh, great, cigars. When did they light those?" Vanessa grumbled, her good mood ebbing.

"Eh, boys." Kelli threw a hand. "Boyd knows he's not getting any tonight, anyway."

"Uh-oh, what'd he do?" Carroll asked playfully. "Forget to iron your socks again?"

Andy and Gwen sat forward in their chairs and laughed heartily at the insult. Even Kelli and Vanessa couldn't keep from joining in.

It was a true rarity for Andy to have this kind of evening with her sisters. Where every one of them was loose and relaxed and no one was passing judgment. Gwen's best friend had since collected Matthew and left, so it was only the Paynes and their significant others on the patio. Andy decided to hell with sizing them up. For the remainder of the weekend, she'd just *be*.

They might've been the dominant excuse for her bringing a date in the first place, but Gage had become more than a stand-in so that she could avoid judgment from her family. She now saw that each of them had their own issues, less concerned with Andy than she'd originally imagined. Gage accepted her, liked her, for who she was. It was past time she accepted *herself*.

"Looks like Gage is abstaining," Estelle pointed out, tipping her chin toward the group of guys. Sure enough, Gage stood, arms folded, unlit cigar cradled between two fingers. He was participating in the conversation with everyone, but not smoking. Interesting.

"That must mean he and Andy have some sexy plans tonight." Gwen elbowed Andy in the arm. "Do tell, sister. How is he?"

"How *big* is he?" Carroll chimed in.

"Girls!" Estelle covered her ears. "I'm not listening to this." Vanessa pulled their mother's hands from her ears and then Estelle said, "Unless you'd like to hear details of your father's—"

"No!" all five sisters called out in unison.

Estelle grinned, pleased that her bluff had worked.

"You don't have to be graphic," Carroll stated.

"But be a *little* graphic." Vanessa leaned forward in her chair. Even Kelli looked curious.

"I'm excusing myself to the ladies' room." Estelle threw her hands into the air and hustled off to the restaurant. When she was gone, Andy's sisters raised expectant eyebrows.

"Gage is...attentive."

"Oh, I love attentive," Carroll said, nodding in support.

"Is he a slow kisser? A deep kisser?" Gwen asked, chin in her hands and elbows on her knees.

"Yes to both," Andy answered, and sighs of delight echoed around her. "I don't know what's going to come next. He goes from kissing my mouth, to my neck, to that part behind my ear."

"I *love* that part." Kelli sat up now, too, her attention on Andy.

"What about the first time you ever had sex?" Vanessa asked on a whisper. "Where was it? How long did you wait?"

"Well...it was...more recently than you might think," Andy said, her tongue loosened from the wine, and yeah, she was caught up in the attention.

"How recent? And where? How did it happen?" Carroll asked rapid-machine-gun-style.

Andy opened her mouth, unsure what would come

out of it when a low male voice interjected, "Whoa, whoa, whoa... What did I walk in on?"

Every one of her sisters sat up, backs straight in their chairs as Gage rounded behind them and aimed accusatory looks at each one.

"Leave you alone for a few minutes, and you're telling all." Hands on Andy's shoulders, Gage kneaded her tight muscles. He'd done a good job of loosening her up earlier, but now that easy-breezy feeling ebbed away.

She shut her eyes, mortified that he'd overheard her. This was why she never allowed herself more than two glasses of wine! She became caught up, the wine an elixir urging the truth from her. She'd forgotten that she had a story to keep up with: a *pretend* boyfriend she was *for real* sleeping with.

How had the lines gotten so blurry?

"Gage. We were just—" she started, lamely.

"You women are worse than those guys over there," he said, but she could hear the smile in his voice, the teasing tone that was good-natured and so *Gage*. "Ready to head back, sweetheart?"

"We noticed you didn't smoke a cigar," Kelli said, crossing her legs. She'd recovered from being busted quicker than any of them. Even Ness looked a bit chagrined.

"Not tonight."

"Oh? Why's that? Plans with Andrea?" Kelli asked.

Gage took Andy's hand and helped her stand. When she faced him, he said, "Yes. I have *many* plans for Andrea tonight."

Thirteen

"That was a close one." Andy had been on the spot in front of her sisters. The jig would've well and truly been up if she'd even hinted at the fact that hers and Gage's first time had been *today*.

"I thought I'd whisk you out of there before you had to make up a story about the first time we had sex. You liked me coming to your rescue." He tossed their suite's key card on the counter where they'd had sex hours earlier, and then he gripped her hips, pulling her in front of him. "Admit it."

He'd been dying to kiss her again all evening, and while he hadn't minded leaving her sisters with something to chew on, out-and-out PDA seemed over-the-top for Andy.

"I did love it." She swept her fingers into his hair and toyed with the curled ends. "You claimed me."

His eyes sought hers, lost in the depths of those earnest blues. Andrea Payne was a woman who was smooth and detached on the outside. A woman who knew what she wanted and how to get it. A woman who, to achieve a goal, would approach a man in a bar and offer him two grand to come with her to a wedding. What she didn't know about herself, and what Gage was trying to show her, was that she was also soft and caring, giving and loving. She was sensitive and demure, and the slightest bit shy, and every one of those attributes did it for him. Especially when they came wrapped in a package of freckles and strawberry hair and blue eyes so bright he could sink into them for days.

He blinked, jerking his chin back in shock. Normally when it came to women he wasn't this…poetic. Could be the cognac. Could be the setting—love was in the air.

Or it could be that he'd been taking this pretend role of boyfriend to real extremes.

He hadn't been a boyfriend in a long, *long* time. The last time he'd escalated to fiancé and that wasn't something he was interested in repeating. When Laura left, he'd felt filleted. Like someone had stripped out his bones and left him a heap of flesh on the floor.

Yeah, no repeats on that, thanks.

"No one would've believed we waited eight months before making love on a countertop at my sister's wedding retreat." She played with his hair some more. "We didn't wait more than a few weeks before we caved."

"Two weeks too long," he admitted, his earlier reminiscing forgotten.

Right now was about *right now.*

He'd didn't typically worry about the future and he'd be damned if he ruined the weekend with it now. He moved her hair over her shoulder. "When you came at me like a lioness in that bar, I'd decided to take you home and damn the consequences."

"Is that so?" She tilted one eyebrow. "What about that cute bartender you'd been flirting with all evening? Did you swap her for me so easily?"

"You were watching me." He narrowed his eyes in accusation.

"I—" Her mouth gaped for a second. "Only between bouts of my date talking incessantly about himself."

"What did you see when you looked across the room at me, Andy?"

"You mean other than an opportunity?"

He smirked at her deflection. "How'd you know the bartender wasn't my girlfriend?"

"I didn't. I…assumed."

"And you also assumed I was a sorry sap in dire need of two thousand dollars."

She squeezed her eyes closed, her cheeks going the sweetest tinge of pink. "I didn't think you needed two thousand dollars." When her eyes reopened, she looked up at him with such raw vulnerability, his heart clutched. "I thought it'd take two thousand dollars to convince you to say yes…to me."

He gripped her chin and lifted her face just enough to keep her eyes on him while he made sure what he said next sank in.

"Honey, I was going to take you home based on one look. Based on you stalking toward me like you wanted to make a meal out of me. And trust me when I say, I have a very good reason for not liking that look on a woman."

"Sounds like a story."

"For another day," he said. "I liked your determination. You saw what you wanted and you were coming to get it. Certainty, *honesty*, is a huge turn-on for me."

"But you said no." Her eyebrows pinched.

"You offered to pay me!" He let out a chortle, his fingers threading in her hair. "Tell me if I'd have offered you the same you would've gladly accepted."

"Oh. No. Of course I wouldn't have… I'd never…" Her fingers came up to cover her lips as she pushed his arms aside. Between her hands she said, "Gage, I'm so sorry I made you feel…cheap."

"You made me feel confused, Andy. Not cheap. In no way should you have ever felt like you couldn't earn a yes from me instead of buying it." He tugged her hands from her mouth and kissed her fingers. "You're worth it."

In the distance of Gage's mind he was aware that this was how he gave women the wrong impression: by being likable. By being honest about what he liked about them. But he couldn't help being likable any more than he could help liking Andy a bit too much. A bit more than common sense suggested he should…

Her hand came to rest on his chest and she gave him a push. "You like me determined, Fleming?" she asked, her voice hard and unyielding.

His lips twitched, but he didn't dare smile. "Yes, ma'am."

At her playful shove, he walked a few steps backward toward the bedroom.

"Good. There are things I want from you," she stated.

"Oh?" He was intrigued as hell. "What things?"

"I want to taste you." Her fingers trickled down his button-down shirt. "I want to feel you hard and heavy in my mouth."

His eyes zoomed in on her plush lips as she—God help him—swiped her bottom lip with her tongue. *Slowly*. His cock gave an insistent twitch from behind his fly.

"Take off your pants," she commanded.

Gage wouldn't allow her to do all the commanding. He had things he wanted to do to her as well. Instead of obeying, he cupped her jaw with both hands and kissed her sweetly. The sweet turned to hard, the hard to long, the long to soft. When he pulled away, she whimpered her protestation at losing his mouth. He took advantage of her being dazed and unbuttoned her pants, sliding his hand into her panties to find her damp and inviting.

Against her parted lips, he whispered, "You first."

Waves of pleasure streaked up her spine as Andy came at Gage's command. He hadn't even taken her pants off yet. Instead, he'd rooted them to the spot on the floor and moved from stroking her to sliding a finger deep inside of her. When a second finger joined the first, her talented wedding date thumbed her clitoris once, twice…and the third time was a charm.

She opened her eyes, her breathing erratic, her palms resting on his shoulders. She might topple over if she didn't hold on to him. But she didn't find a pleased smile on Gage's face, no. He was all heat and seriousness when he lowered his lips to hers. His whisper was hot, his breath coasting over her lips when he said, "That was beautiful to watch."

She'd never been with anyone like him. Someone so confident and easygoing, and…well, who *liked her*, quite frankly. She'd never liked someone as much as he liked her back, so the mutual attraction was brand-new.

"Thank you," she breathed.

That brought forth his brilliant smile. "Show, don't tell, Ms. Payne."

She bit the inside of her cheek, knowing what he was referring to. She'd made him a promise. Reaching for his hard-on, she massaged him and earned a deep kiss for her efforts. In a blur of movement, Gage maneuvered them backward into the bedroom while keeping their lips sealed. She unfastened his pants as he tore at her shirt, leaving them in a pile on the floor.

When he reached the bed, she undid his shirt one button at a time, revealing his chest and smoothing her fingers over the scant hair whorling around flat male nipples, dusting his clenching abs, and finally to that trail of hair that disappeared into his black boxers.

"I've never been so excited to have someone naked before," she said, half surprised she'd said it aloud.

"Honey, have at it." He thumbed her cheek as a deep breath lifted his shoulders and broadened his bare chest. Anticipation hung heavy in the air between them. She let it linger for a few agonizing seconds and then dropped to her knees and tugged on his boxers.

"Look at me when you do it." He wound her long hair around his fist and held it away from her face.

She licked her lips and his hips surged forward. He was suddenly intense, not the same playful guy from earlier. She couldn't wait to experience his flavor, and was trying to decide if she would linger at the head or pepper the shaft with kisses.

She started with a sweet kiss to the tip. His answering groan spurred her on, bolstering her confidence and making her sit a little taller. When she opened her mouth to accommodate him, she did as he asked and turned her eyes up to his…

Gage typically held off coming by reciting the last quarter's sales numbers in silence, but with Andy's eyes zeroed in on him, he couldn't concoct a single thought that didn't involve her. On her knees, her fingers lightly tickling his balls, and those blue, blue eyes fastened to him and holding him hostage.

He locked his thigh muscles as she took him deeply into her mouth again and again. He didn't think of sales numbers or baseball stats, or any other helpful distraction that might keep his release at bay. He didn't want to miss a single second of Andy making love to him with her mouth.

She was a glorious sight. Her pink-tipped breasts bare as she knelt there in nothing but a pair of black panties. The way she gripped his shaft with nails painted the same color red as her shirt had been.

Mercy.

She'd be his undoing. He was sure of it. He wasn't sure what that meant yet, and he wasn't sure he would've changed a damn thing if he'd known before now, but she was not unlike a female praying mantis. He was willingly, gladly allowing himself to be devoured.

Thoughts of cannibal insects and his imminent doom faded away when she swirled her tongue and took him deep. His hand that had been holding her hair out of the way tightened into a fist and he let out a grunt, followed by a plea.

"Can't…believe I'm…saying this…"

She let him go before slowly taking him deep again and his brain blanked. Seriously, he had nothing in his head during the next slick slide, but his memory returned when the telltale tingle of his pending orgasm shimmied up his spine.

"Stop, sweetheart. I need to be inside you. *Now*."

He watched as she let him go, his length slipping from her wet, parted mouth.

God.

Damn.

He blinked. Hard. Resetting his brain and hopefully gaining a modicum of restraint. He lifted her by the elbows, helping himself to exploring her plush mouth when it reached his.

"You are so hot it's ridiculous," he panted. "You could lead me around with that move, you know that?"

She offered a pleased grin as he worked her panties down her legs. "Does that mean you're my sex slave now?"

"Yes," he said without hesitation. Though he didn't like the idea of any woman leading him around by the pecker, for Andy—for this weekend—he could make an exception and forgive himself for it later.

"On your back, beautiful. Let's do this properly."

She lay down and pushed herself up the bed, gloriously naked—all that smooth skin exposed for his eyes and his twitching fingers. He slid his hand from her hip to her ribs and back up to her breasts.

"So much better." He kissed her lightly. "No complicated countertops or vertical maneuvering."

"Yeah." Her smile the slightest bit shaky. Before he could work out what that meant, she said, "Condom."

"Right." Right! Wow. Where was his head? He'd been consumed with being inside her and totally forgotten about protection. *Rookie move, Fleming.*

Again that distant alarm rang, a little louder than before. It hinted that he was in deeper than he'd intended, but that was stupid. This was a temporary arrangement between them—they were completely compatible physically. No reason not to enjoy themselves.

Repeatedly.

He retrieved a condom from his wallet and rolled it on, returning to Andy. Then he lifted her leg and lined up with her center, enjoying teasing her. Enjoying watching her hands clench the sheets into a wad, her lips parting in anticipation.

"You want me, Strawberry?" he asked.

She didn't take him to task for the nickname, only hastily nodded.

He didn't tease either of them any longer, thrusting inside of her in one mind-melting slide. She cried out, her pleasure infusing the air with a scent not unlike the cinnamon of her perfume.

He repeated the action again, again, until she locked her legs around him and cried out with wild abandon. He lost track of his voice as well, especially when he came on what would qualify in most countries as a roar and collapsed on top of her. His entire body was buzzing, his head detached, a slight layer of sweat sticky between them.

He returned to earth when Andy's fingers found his hair. A move that was already becoming familiar to him, and was unique to her.

That caused another alarm to break through the haze of his orgasm.

But he ignored that one as well.

Fourteen

Gage woke to the telltale clicking of computer keys, his head swimming through a seascape of dreams. He opened his eyelids a crack to notice two things: one, it was still dark outside, and two, Andy was sitting up in bed next to him, laptop on her lap, naked breasts highlighted in the bluish light emanating from the screen.

He stretched his hand across the bed—king-size, so he had a way to go—and brushed her thigh with an open palm. She started, jerking her head over to him before flashing him a grin. And flashing him, period, considering the movement also shifted her long hair from where it covered her breasts and out peeked a nipple.

"What are you doing?" he asked, his voice sleepy and craggy.

"Working," she whispered. "Did I wake you?"

"Yes." He sat up in bed next to her, propping a pillow behind his back. He pressed a kiss to her shoulder. *Mmm.* She smelled good. He lingered on the second kiss and she sighed, a soft sound from her throat, before giving in and turning her head for a kiss. A kiss he almost gave her.

"Hang on." He wandered out of the suite and into the bathroom, using the facilities before washing his hands, face, and finally scrubbing his teeth. He wasn't going to kiss her long and slow if he had dragon breath, that was for damn sure.

When he emerged, she was standing in the living room, bare-ass-naked. "If you're going to brush your teeth, then I have to, too." She seemed inconvenienced by this, but he was glad to see that the laptop on the bed was closed.

He climbed back into bed and glanced at the clock, doing a double take. When Andy meandered back into their shared room, teeth brushed, he pointed at the digital readout. "It's barely five a.m."

"I know."

"Does the word *vacation* mean nothing to you?" He rarely saw the other side of six o'clock in the morning. Whenever he'd tried to start his day earlier than that, he'd met it grouchy and groggy. He was still groggy, but his grouchiness had been replaced by another feeling entirely, considering Andy was crawling toward him in bed, her breasts shifting temptingly with every move she made, her hair tickling up his body.

She rested on him, chest to chest, and Gage cupped

her bottom, his grogginess dissipating when she leaned in to kiss him slowly.

"I'm an early riser."

He pushed his pelvis into hers, his arousal making itself known despite what time it was. "Me, too, but never this early."

Not that he usually had a reason to wake hard and ready. Rare was the occasion a woman stayed over. And on the off chance she had, he pretended to be fast asleep until she left so they didn't have to do this dance. Many, *many* lines were being crossed with Andy, and while he knew that wasn't cause for a panic attack, he reminded himself not to get used to it.

"What time's the rehearsal?" he asked around a yawn. "Early, right?"

"Ten o'clock."

In the morning, he knew. Evidently Gwen and Garrett had opted to rehearse for the wedding the morning of the wedding, which wasn't typical. He remembered that from the quick scan of the itinerary.

"That gives us several hours," Andy purred before pressing a kiss to his shoulder. Then his neck. When she opened her mouth at the base of his throat, he slid his arms to her back and squeezed.

"I need my beauty sleep," he joked.

"Sex first, then you can sleep, princess." She nipped his bottom lip and soothed the twinge with a kiss.

"There is some serious role reversal going on here," he pointed out. "I don't like it."

"You don't like not being in charge?"

"Correct." He was all-the-way hard now, the languid, teasing kisses and verbal sparring turning him on regardless of what ungodly time of morning it was. "I have a better idea."

He reversed their positions, rolling Andy to her back and sliding down her body as he laid kisses here and there. Her eyes widened with excitement.

"What are you doing?" The question burst from her like a bottle rocket, capping with her stopping him when he began kissing a line down the center of her breasts.

"Making sure you go back to sleep when I'm through with you," he mumbled against her skin, shaking off her hands to kiss her flat belly.

"Gage." She clamped her legs together, her hands returning to his hair. He gave her his attention and that was when she shook her head. "You don't want to do that."

"Oh, but I do." He removed one of her hands from his head and kissed her palm. "You touch my hair a lot."

The panicky expression gave way to a shaky grin.

"I don't remember any woman I've been with who played with my hair the way you do."

"Sorry."

"Not a complaint. And right now a big turn-on." He put her hand back on his head. "Pull when I do something you like and I'll keep doing it until you explode." He gave her a wink, licking a line just under her belly button before moving to her thigh and kissing there, too.

Her clean scent hit him, musky and inviting. He absolutely could not wait to taste her. To make her scream his name.

"But…"

With a sigh, he raised his face from the cradle of her thighs.

"You're sure?"

"Andy, haven't you ever done this before?" A rhetorical question, because surely...

But she slowly shook her head, and in the sparse light from the digital clock he could see her cheeks darken with color. He had no idea how that was possible, or what dickweeds she'd dated who didn't take the time, energy and effort to satisfy her—but...

He knew of one, didn't he?

He kept his eyes on hers as he lowered his lips to just above her center. "Step one—" he licked her seam, thrilling when desire bloomed in her eyes and her mouth dropped open "—let me do all the work."

Shifting her so that her knees were resting on his shoulders, he opened her to him. "Step two—" he placed another reverent lick to the heart of her "—instructions are encouraged. Faster, slower, left, right, that kind of thing."

She bit her lip—to keep away a smile, he was guessing. Her shoulders had come down from her ears, and he wondered if that was because he'd just made it clear she had no need for performance anxiety.

"Step three—" instead of one lick, he delivered several in rapid succession, loving the way she thrust upward toward his seeking tongue "—enjoy yourself. This is all for you."

Her fingers were in his hair, seeking, pulling and pushing or a combination of all three when he went to work. When she was close, she rewarded him with a high cry and he doubled down on his efforts, concentrating on that one spot in particular designed to make her lose her mind. She never gave him instructions but she never had to. Soon she was coming, clenching around his fingers, which he'd added to help her get there, and crying his name on a weak, sated shout.

Hell.

Yes.

He kissed her hip bone and then her ribs, placed a loving peck on each of her nipples and then suckled her earlobe when he reached it. Her heartbeat was erratic, her breathing labored and her eyes closed.

"Wow" was the first word she said. And Gage, who'd meant that exploration as a precursor to some really great morning sex, decided he'd let her ride this wave into oblivion.

"Sleep well, Strawberry." He gave her one last kiss and she grunted what might've been a word if he hadn't rendered her every muscle useless. Proud of himself, he rolled over, his erection protesting. He ignored it. She needed that—worse than he'd originally known, apparently—and he'd been the first to give it to her. That special sort of release when you're the center of the attention—the very attention she'd given him without hesitation last night.

In the dark, she began to lightly snore and he smiled in wonderment at the creature who'd brought him here, bedded him and confused him constantly.

Who was this woman?

And how, in all of his years of folly and dating, had he never met another like her?

Andy showed up for the casual brunch rehearsal wearing a light floral dress rather than the navy blue bridesmaid's dress she'd purchased for Gwen's navy-and-red-themed wedding. Gwen had eschewed the traditional rehearsal *dinner* for a casual brunch rehearsal, which was being held in a tented-off area in view of the lake.

The sky was heavy with clouds, but the weather was warm. The app on Andy's phone showed the skies clearing by noon, and nothing but sun after, which was good news for Gwen and Garrett's 4:00 p.m. ceremony.

Gage accompanied Andy to the rehearsal even though she'd assured him he didn't have to come. He didn't need to rehearse for anything. He'd insisted, though, saying he'd better regain his strength and *"have something other than you for breakfast,"* which made her remember how completely he'd spoiled her this morning.

After he'd successfully tranquilized her by going down on her, she'd slipped off into the most pleasant sleep of her life before waking him an hour later in much the same fashion. The sex had been electrifying and gratifying, and yet lazy and languid, the way morning sex should be.

She'd ridden him, her hair tickling her back, and he'd held onto her hips, lifting to meet her with each languid thrust. It was the kind of sex a girl could get used to, but that thought made her melancholy, so she'd ignored it all morning. If there was one clear boundary line between her and Gage it was that they shouldn't get too used to being together.

"I'm grabbing a bite to eat that's guaranteed to be less satisfying than you," Gage whispered in her ear.

She ducked her head, suddenly shy at the copious

attention. He placed a kiss on her temple before leaving her to her sister Gwen, who appeared uncharacteristically nervous.

Uh-oh.

"Hey. Everything okay?" Andy asked.

"No." Gwen's gaze flitted left, then right. "Carroll is my maid of honor, and Garrett's best friend is Kenny, so that worked out perfectly. But you're my bridesmaid and so is Amber, and Amber is dating Matthew, who is your ex."

"Right," Andy said, waiting for the other shoe to drop.

"Garrett doesn't really like Matthew."

Andy didn't really like Matthew, either.

"But he's in the wedding party. Because I love Amber and she's in love with Matthew and wanted him to be her partner. So I talked Garrett into it, which makes me feel awful…but worse than that—" Gwen winced "—I didn't warn you about Matthew being here. I'm a giant coward."

Andy tracked her eyes past Gwen over to where the wedding party was gathered near the wedding arch. Granted, she didn't like Matthew any more than Garrett did, but she wasn't going to ruin her sister's day. "I'm sure it'll be fine, Gwen. We've survived this weekend so far without incident."

Except him referring to her as Ice Queen. But Gage had been there to stand up for her.

"He said you called him and he told you he'd be here."

Andy stiffened. She'd called Matthew to ask him to be her stand-in date, in a fit of insanity, apparently, but luckily never had to ask. Matthew had interrupted and bragged about attending with another date—Gwen's best friend, Amber.

"I did… I did call him. I was curious about how he was doing. It was a random whim," Andy lied.

"I should have been the one to tell you—to warn you. It'd been so long since you two dated… I guess I didn't give it much thought." Gwen pressed her lips together before adding, "Are you sure you're not mad at me for not warning you?"

Andy palmed her youngest sister's shoulder, relieved Gwen wasn't instead suspicious over the reason that Andy had called Matthew in the first place. "No, Gwen. I'm not the least bit mad."

"Good." Gwen's shoulders sagged in relief. "You're walking with Garrett's good friend Jon, who arrived this morning. He's in the blue shirt."

Andy spotted the slender, smiling man in khakis and a golf shirt. "Okay."

"Don't be mad about this, either, but I sort of told him you were single."

"Gwen!"

"I didn't expect you to bring a date! If he hits on you, break it to him gently!"

Andy sighed. Just what she needed. First, she'd barely scrounged a date for this wedding, then she'd learned Matthew would darken the wedding's doorstep, and now she was sleeping with her pretend boyfriend *and* had another suitor asking if she was available? She'd never had so many man problems in her entire life.

One more look at Gwen showed that she wasn't her normal happy-go-lucky self. This must be what the pre-wedding bridal jitters looked like on her. Kelli had had an outburst about her bouquet containing the wrong kind of roses, Ness had dissolved into tears when her flower girl refused to wear the tiara that matched her own and Carroll had done a shot of peppermint schnapps to ease her last-second nerves before she walked down the aisle.

"I'll let him down gently," Andy assured her.

"Thank you." Gwen beamed. "I'm getting married."

"You are!" Andy couldn't help smiling back at her youngest sister. She was enjoying herself so much now that she was here. Andy had Gage to thank for that. He seemed to be the common denominator in every moment she'd been at ease. "I'm so, *so* happy for you and Garrett."

Gwen embraced her in a tight squeeze that made Andy's eyes watery. "I'm so happy for you and Gage. I know Ness and Mom can be complete pains in the rear about pairing you off, but they want what's best for you deep down on the inside."

Andy hoisted a brow. "It must be buried deeper than the mines of Moria."

Gwen giggled, loving the *Lord of the Rings* reference, as Andy knew she would. "Thanks, Andy. I appreciate you being understanding."

"Sure thing." She followed Gwen to the wedding arch, toward Matthew and the stranger she'd be paired with in the wedding, and drew back her shoulders in determination.

She could do this.

And maybe it was better if she did. She'd used Gage as her security blanket for long enough. Andy could handle this part on her own.

Better get used to it, a tiny voice warned.

Soon she'd be back in Seattle and their bout of pretending would be over. But their physical connection wasn't pretend for her at all. She wondered if it was for Gage, or if, like her, he was steeling himself for the end.

Fifteen

Around noon the clouds swept aside like curtains, parting to reveal the sunshine. By the time Gage made his way to the wedding area, the grass was dry and the day warm but not too hot.

He was invited to sit with the remaining Payne sisters who weren't included in the wedding. He overheard Ness say she'd begged off, not wanting "to deal with another useless bridesmaid's dress."

Not that he'd ever accuse any woman of being an "Ice Queen" but he wasn't entirely sure how Andy had earned that moniker over Vanessa.

Gage took the seat next to Boyd on one of the white plastic folding chairs arranged in rows. He turned to smile at the tiny flower girl walking down the aisle beside Carroll, who was helping the little girl throw petals. The tot probably had no idea why she was dressed in a white confection and all eyes were on her.

Next came the bridesmaids, and Gage turned expectantly to see Andy. She'd left him in the room, her dress in a bag tossed over her arm, and promised to see him at the wedding. There'd been an awkward moment when she'd debated whether she should kiss him goodbye or not, and then she had. Just a quick peck on the side of his mouth. He'd wished her good luck.

The sight of her now stole the moisture from his mouth. She was…ethereal.

The navy blue dress was knee-length, the sleeves designed to reveal her creamy shoulders. Her hair was pulled back on one side, the strawberry blonde color a stunning accent to the blue. The photographer leaned out of an aisle to snap a photo and Andy smiled, her plush lips shining with sparkly pink gloss. When she caught sight of Gage, her smile stayed but turned demure, the joy in her blue eyes zapping him where he sat.

Then she walked past him to take her place up front, and Amber followed. By the time the music changed to introduce the bride, Gage didn't want to take his eyes from his date. And when a white-dressed Gwen strode down the aisle to take her place next to Garrett, Gage felt his forehead break into a sweat.

Could've been you.

He'd been to weddings since his engagement with Laura had imploded. He'd always had a date, so that part wasn't new. He'd never pictured himself in the role of the groom, with a bride in white coming toward him down a long aisle.

Until right now.

Gripping his hands in front of him, he forced himself to take a few long breaths. When Boyd eyed him curiously, Gage gave him a pained I'm-fine smile. Eyebrows bowed in sympathy, Boyd patted Gage's back gruffly and then turned to watch the ceremony.

What was that about? What was the back-pat and that knowing smile supposed to reinforce? Gage swiped his brow again. When it came time for the prayer he ducked his head, but his eyes and thoughts stayed on Andy.

Andrea Payne was a puzzle, like Kenny had said.

But Kenny had also said that when Gage and Andrea were together, Kenny could see the full picture. That picture spread out before Gage now, even though he didn't quite know what to make of it.

He saw Andy in his future.

That wasn't something he'd been able to say of any woman besides Laura. But he was enamored with Andy in a way he'd never been with any woman—and that *included* Laura.

In the midst of pretending to be Andy's boyfriend, Gage was feeling particularly boyfriend-like. He was going against several rules he'd set up to protect himself, including endangering the bachelor pact he and Reid were still upholding.

Gage wouldn't muster up a version of a wedding of his own—lest he throw up on his and Boyd's shoes—but he could safely state that when he and Andy returned to Seattle, he'd like to keep seeing her.

Thing was, he wasn't 100 percent sure she wanted to keep seeing him.

So.

That was new.

Typically, it was the woman he was dating who was leaning on him a little too hard. Crowding into his space and wanting the "more" he couldn't give her. Meanwhile here he was, literally a few days into this…fantasy romance, and starting to feel a whole host of things he shouldn't.

Particularly when Andy rested her hand on the arm of the groomsman she'd been paired with and they both smiled at the camera.

If Gage were to let this affair end, he imagined Andy would eventually find a man worthy of her time. They couldn't all be duds. Maybe even after she and Gage split, the nice-guy-looking groomsman would call her up.

"Hey, Andrea. You remember me? Pencil Neck from Gwen's wedding? I thought we could get together sometime for a bland dinner before I try to impress you with a few of my lame bedroom moves."

Gage felt his lip curl at the idea of another guy trying to spend time with Andy. Possessive was another trait he'd never had to contend with. But here it was, as gritty and basal as he'd ever imagined.

Whenever he looked at Andrea Payne, a bolt of certainty shocked his gut with a single word.

Mine.

He wanted her, and he'd had her.

But he hadn't had *enough* of her.

Even though previously he'd decided beyond a shadow of a doubt that he would never get married or engaged.

Was there an in-between? Was Andy the kind of woman who would settle for some but not all?

He was beginning to think he wasn't that kind of

guy. That he was instead the kind of guy who'd like to get married someday. That he was the kind of guy who'd like to have a family and a wife and buy a house with a yard he had to mow.

But only if that future included Andy.

So.

Yeah.

What the hell was he supposed to do with *that*?

Thankfully the tradition of a formal wedding party dance wasn't one Gwen and Garrett kept. The happy couple finished their dance as husband and wife and then the DJ played a song about single women that would inevitably herald the bouquet toss. Andy settled in at the round table decorated with red roses in navy vases, her hand in Gage's, content not to move. Until…

"Get up there, girl," Kelli goaded.

"Me?" Andy shook her head. "I'm not single. I'm here with Gage."

"Yes, but you're not married to Gage. Or engaged to Gage." A small frown marred her sister's forehead. "Are you?"

"No." Andy shook her head and met Gage's eyes. He looked slightly green and she could imagine why. Pretending to be her boyfriend was one thing. Pretending to be her fiancé was a whole other level of OMG. "But I'm not single."

"That's not how it works." Kelli grabbed Andy's hand and dragged her to the dance floor, where Amber was already boogying to the music.

Andy stood behind Amber and the other four girls who were on the stage, arms in the air. Gwen searched the crew of available bachelorettes and Andy quickly shook her head. Gwen smirked, slapped her hand over her eyes and threw the bouquet high.

It arced toward Amber, but the toss was high and Amber was about six inches shorter than Andy. Either the gorgeous bouquet of blue roses with red ribbon hit the dance floor and exploded into a shower of petals, thereby ruining her youngest sister's day, or...

Andy held out her hands in a show of an attempt. The bouquet landed prettily in her palms like Gwen had aimed directly for her.

Cheers rang out and Andy held her prize overhead, her headshake a combination of chagrin and *that-figures*.

But when she caught sight of Gage applauding, she felt happy she'd gone along with this farce anyway. Just to have him here with her—just to be in his company. Even if it was only for the weekend.

The DJ called for the single guys as Andy stepped from the dance floor, and this time it was not Kelli but Garrett calling to the men who'd rather not stand up and catch Gwen's garter.

Garrett shoved Jon onto the dance floor as a random smattering of single guys shuffled into their spots, beers in hand. Andy tried to hold Garrett off when he angled for Gage, but Garrett only winked at her.

"Sorry, Andrea. He has to make an attempt. Especially since you have the bouquet." When Garrett slapped Gage on the back, she also heard him say, "You don't want Jon slipping a garter onto your girl's thigh, now do you?"

Gage sent a heated glance over his shoulder at

Andy and flames licked along her body like he'd touched her instead.

Saucy, silly burlesque music piped from the speakers as Garrett shimmied a garter belt from high on his bride's thigh. He slid it down the remainder of Gwen's leg with his teeth, which made everyone cheer and clap except Abe Payne, who covered his eyes when he received a few elbows to the ribs.

"Okay, gentlemen!" Garrett called out. "Who's next? Hey! Hands out of your pockets." After calling out a few of his buddies, Garrett flipped the garter into the crowd like a slingshot, and Jon made a hearty reach for it. He had a few inches on Gage, but Gage made a play for it, launching himself higher by using Jon's shoulder as leverage and snatching the garter out of midair.

Andy applauded when Gage sauntered over, spinning the garter around his finger as several of the guys patted his back.

"All he needed was the right motivation," Garrett shouted as he grabbed a chair and dragged it onto the dance floor.

"Come on, beautiful." Gage offered his hand to Andy. "Let's do this."

She tucked her palm into his. His easygoing attitude had shifted slightly. He was still fun-loving Gage, but a ribbon of seriousness threaded through him as he sat her on the chair and she lifted her leg. His smile was there, his silliness as he verbally urged the crowd on while he slid the garter up her leg, but she couldn't escape the idea that something had changed within him without her knowing. Especially when he tugged her skirt down, helped her stand and asked her to dance as the fast beat slowed into the next ballad.

Couples joined them on the floor and Andy rested her arms on Gage's shoulders as they began to sway.

"Sorry about that." She forced an eye roll even though she wasn't very sorry at all. "I appreciate you defending my honor, though."

"No way was I going to allow Jon—or Matthew—to win that prize and touch even an inch of your leg with their grubby paws."

She giggled. "All my life I've never known a man to be possessive over me, Gage. I think maybe I was lowballing you with my offer of two grand. You're worth much more."

His smile fell, and again she felt as if he was more serious than before. He pushed her hair off her neck, tracing the line from her collarbone to her shoulder. "Have I told you how good you look in this dress?"

"Thank you."

He had. At the start of the reception, when they had parted ways, her bridesmaid chores complete.

"I'm glad you asked me to be your date," Gage said, sneaking a look around to make sure no one was near them. "And for allowing me to share your bed. I have a proposition for you in return."

"Oh?" She bit the inside of her lip, a parade of naughty possibilities lining up to conga through her brain. Would he suggest sex somewhere public, but hidden in shadows? Maybe he wanted to make love by moonlight on the boat. Or maybe, when they went back to the room, he would get a bucket of ice and tease a cube along her inner thighs…

"When we return to Seattle, what if we don't stop?"

She swayed in his arms, not understanding his meaning. "Don't stop what?"

"Any of it. You coming to my place. Me to yours." He turned them in a smooth circle. "I can't promise opportunities for garters or dancing, but the rest of it—the meals, the dates, the waking you up by going down on you—" he whispered, leaning in "—why stop now?"

Sixteen

Andy had been putting off thinking about life back in Seattle until after the wedding was over. But the weekend was winding down quickly, wasn't it? It was nearing the end of the time she and Gage would spend together and now that she allowed herself to think about what that meant for them...well, *not* seeing him didn't sound even a little appealing.

"You want to keep seeing me?" She was still trying to wrap her brain around that. It wasn't a typical discussion she'd had with her mediocre dates and underwhelming boyfriend prospects.

"We're good together, Andy. I didn't come here expecting...this." He raised their linked hands to gesture around them. "To be this comfortable with you. Especially in this scenario."

"Hmm. You're going to need to explain that." He'd

hinted that there was a story from his past before, but he hadn't shared it. By her estimations she had him right where she wanted him.

"Wondered if I could escape explanation." He sighed heavily.

"You can," she told him, quickly changing her tune. "You don't owe me anything. But since we're planning on *not stopping*, it would be nice to know you a bit better. Beyond the biblical sense, I mean." She winked and he chuckled, settling into their dancing rhythm with ease.

"Since you've just agreed to my terms, I suppose I could indulge you with a few details of my sordid past."

"Oh, sordid. That's a good beginning to any story."

He took a deep breath before he spoke, like there was still a part of him that was resisting. "I was engaged when I was a junior in college."

"Young."

"Quite." He lifted a sardonic eyebrow. "Laura and I…ended our engagement."

"Code for she dumped you."

"Precisely. After that engagement ended, I decided this—" he jerked his chin to indicate the wedding guests, tent and the bride and groom themselves "—wasn't for me. By then there was a pact issued by my buddies that we'd agree never to marry."

"Which buddies?" But she had a guess.

"Reid and Flynn."

"Ha! But aren't Flynn and Sabrina…?"

"Yeah, they are. He broke the contract, but after seeing them together it made sense. You've seen them. It's undeniable how they feel about each other."

"It's pretty obvious," she agreed.

"Anyway, he's been married before, and once the divorce was underway, he was the one to reinstate the pact. He was upset, as well as he should've been since his now ex-wife cheated on him with his brother."

Andy sucked air through her teeth. "Yowch. Tell me there was nothing that ugly behind the ending of your engagement with Laura."

"No, nothing like that," he said easily enough that she believed him. "We were young. It wouldn't have lasted."

The music faded into another slow song, and they kept on swaying.

"So what is your modus operandi with dating now? Or do you exclusively bail out women in need of wedding dates so long as they pay your room and travel?"

"Believe it or not, you are my first. Typically, I just…date. I don't have any weird rules or anything, but I don't ask for more. And if she does…" He shook his head.

"So you sleep with these women and then leave a trail of broken hearts when they start wanting more?"

"First of all, there aren't that many of them and few leave brokenhearted, so stop making me sound like a lothario." He tugged her so that they were dancing cheek to cheek and lowered his lips to her ear. "Secondly, you didn't ask for more. I did."

He pulled away and pegged her with a look that said, *There you go.*

Andy digested that information, feeling like it was substantial in a way that it wasn't before.

"You haven't wanted more with the women you've

dated since college, but now, after only a weekend with me, you know you do?"

"I know I'm not ready to stop talking to you. Or kissing you. Or sharing a bed with you. So I guess my answer is yes. After this weekend, I *know* I'm not through with you."

There it was. Out loud.

Right about now he should be shaking and nervous the way he'd been when he was watching the wedding procession and eyeing Andy like she might be the cause of his pending breakdown.

But he didn't feel that way. He felt like pulling her closer and inhaling her cinnamon scent.

So he did.

He clasped her back and held her to his chest and let his lips hover just over hers. Her fingers wrapped around his neck, and when she slid them into his hair, he had to smile.

"I'm not sure what to say about any of this except the truth." Vulnerability danced in her eyes but she didn't look away. His brave girl.

"Hit me. I can handle it."

"I've never had a relationship like this with anyone."

"You mean fake for the sake of your family?" he teased.

"No." But she smiled like he'd intended. "I trust you, Gage. Maybe more than I should, but I'm acting on instinct whenever I'm with you. Which is probably why I haven't denied myself much where you're concerned."

"That makes me sound like an indulgence and I really, *really* like that."

"You are an indulgence. And I never indulge."

He'd bet. Every lean curve on her not only reflected good genes but also suggested a rigid workout regimen and being mindful of every calorie she ate.

"Especially in the bedroom," she whispered before covering his lips with a soft kiss.

"Check, please," he muttered, only half kidding.

"I'm going to visit the ladies' room." The song ended and the couples on the dance floor moved away. Perfect timing.

"I'm going to the bar, where I'll grab a water and dump it over my head." When she laughed, he added, "And down my pants."

"I'll meet you over there."

But when they parted, he didn't want to let her go, holding her hand until the last possible moment when her fingers slipped from his.

"Sap," he muttered to himself, quelling the panicky feeling in his belly before it bloomed in his chest.

So, he'd asked to keep seeing her. So what? He didn't promise her forever. He could be with Andy and not end up like Flynn and Sabrina.

Gage wasn't done with her yet, and that was enough for him. They were in a safe space to continue riding the middle until it made sense not to be together any more. There was no reason to believe what they had would doom him to forever.

And there was no way to deny that her agreement to keep doing what they were doing made him damn glad he'd brought it up.

Andy walked from the frigid air-conditioned building into the warm, welcome summer breeze of the tent.

She moved to her table to grab her purse and found her sister Vanessa cradling a half-full glass of white wine and looking unhappy, which seemed to be her normal expression. Ness had always been a serious sort. Andy had that in common with her sister, but she wasn't pessimistic, as evidenced by the conversation she'd just had with Gage.

He wanted more. She wanted more. It wasn't a bad way to strike a bargain, either—he'd held her on the dance floor while telling her he'd suffered an ill-fated engagement. And that pact. She'd have made a similar deal with her girlfriends if she'd come that close to matrimony and then had her heart broken.

Andy took a swig from her water glass, lingering next to Ness for a moment.

"Everything all right?" She probably shouldn't ask, but she loved Vanessa, grumpy or no.

"It's always like that in the beginning," her sister responded darkly. Ness gestured with her wineglass to Gwen and Garrett, who were all smiles while dancing to a swing song. "The infatuation and love…and *blindness*. Then a few years go by and what's left is disillusionment and disappointment."

Andy followed Ness's gaze to where Alec stood chatting at the bar with Kenny and Gage, the three of them looking chummy. Andy lowered into the white folding chair next to her sister and leaned in. "Are you and Alec okay?"

Ness's mouth hardened into a flat line. For a moment she looked as if she might cry, but she blinked and jerked her face around, her expression flat but still pretty.

"I don't mean this in an unkind way, Andrea,"

Ness said, and Andy felt her back stiffen with dread. "But what you have with Gage is fleeting. So enjoy him. Enjoy the sex. The rapt excitement whenever you two lock eyes. But don't become entrenched. Don't put yourself in the position of being in a relationship you can't escape. And whatever you do, don't involve paperwork."

"We're…not planning to" was all that Andy could muster as a response.

"Save yourself." Ness finished the remaining wine in her glass and stood. "I'm getting a refill. Want one?"

Andy shook her head, shocked by…well, pretty much everything her sister had just said.

She'd thought Ness and Alec were doing fine. Thought they were happy, even. Granted, Andy hadn't seen them together much this weekend.

A niggle of doubt crept forward. Ness wasn't wrong. Even if one does make it to the altar, the ultimate step in any relationship, everything could still fall apart. And if that was the case, what could any of them count on? She stole a glance at Garrett and Gwen. How long would they be happy?

How long will Gage and I be happy?

Another peek over at Alec proved there was more under the surface than Andy had previously noticed. His smile fell when he met his wife's glare across the tent, his shoulders lifting as if bracing for bad news. Ness approached the bartender to order and Alec curtly smiled at Gage and Kenny, excusing himself before walking off in the opposite direction.

"Oh, Vanessa." Andy sagged in her seat, sad for both her sister and brother-in-law.

They'd been married, what, five years? Six? Wasn't that the point when you could relax in a relationship? Weren't things supposed to get better and better? A closer look at Kelli and Boyd showed they were having no qualms about their own marriage, slow-dancing despite a fast song playing. Even Carroll, who was shimmying with Amber, paused to blow Kenny a kiss that he pretended to catch in his fist. And obviously, Gwen and Garrett were at the peak of happiness today.

Gage parted from Kenny with a wave and walked toward Andy, his sights set on her. He held a glass of whiskey—or some kind of brown liquid—with a single, large ice cube floating in it.

"Danced out?" he asked as he sat next to her.

"Just…resting." She didn't want to air Ness's dirty laundry. It wasn't her story to tell.

"You sure?" He swept her hair aside and kissed her bare shoulder.

She wasn't sure. Not really. But at the same time she wasn't willing to mire herself in her siblings' problems. What would come of Andy and Gage remained to be seen.

They weren't five or six years into a relationship potentially circling the drain. Hell, they hadn't even put a timeframe on what they had. Continuing to see each other back in Seattle might not last a month.

She wasn't willing to stop kissing him or sleeping with him or enjoying him just because the clock struck midnight on Gwen and Garrett's wedding. No matter what the future brought.

"I'm positive," she said instead of sharing her tumultuous thoughts.

She stole a kiss from Gage, letting her lips linger over his, palming his scruffy jaw and then slipping her fingers into the open placket of his shirt.

There was one surefire way to dissolve the worry Ness had planted in the back of Andy's mind, and that was to do what she and Gage were best at doing.

By the time she ended the kiss, he was on the literal edge of his seat, his breaths hectic and erratic.

"Want to get out of here for a few minutes, have some fun, and then sneak back in and eat some cake?" she asked in her best sex-kitten voice.

"Hell, yeah, I do." He stood and pulled her with him, thrusting her purse into her arms. "Lead the way."

Seventeen

Gage pressed a kiss to the left of Andy's spine, then to the right of it, continuing the line of kisses as he drew the zipper on her dress up, up, up until she was dressed.

She sighed, contented, and admittedly sort of lost. Not literally. They might've stolen off to the woods for a quickie disguised as a nature walk, but they weren't far from the festivities. She could see the lights twinkling from the tent and hear the faint sounds of the band playing.

"That was a first," she said when Gage kissed her shoulder.

"Outdoor sex?" He scooted closer to where she sat in the grass and wrapped his arm around her waist. "I like hearing that."

"What about you?" She shifted to face him, her

legs damp from the dew. Now that night had fallen and the sun was down, the humidity sitting in the air had fallen to the ground. She recognized her error in asking when a firm line found his lips. "Oh. I guess... Never mind."

"Not what you think, Strawberry." He tucked her hair behind one ear.

She'd worn a clip holding that side up earlier but had no idea where it'd disappeared to since her and Gage's...*dalliance*. Having sex outside should've felt needy and shallow, but it had been deeper to her.

"The truth is I'm experiencing a few first times with you, too," he said. "You're different."

She opened her mouth to give him a snarky "I know," but he cut her off with a finger to her lips.

"Ah-ah. Your differences are all good ones. When I'm with you, it's not about the setting or the act." He tipped her chin. "It's about what it feels like to be with you. Like I can't get enough."

Nervous at his admission, she swallowed. "Don't go endangering your pact now." The mention of him never being serious with a woman was supposed to ease her nerves and his, too.

"The pact? You think you're in danger of being proposed to?" He canted one eyebrow and gave her an easy smile.

"God, no. What was the catalyst for Flynn reinstating it, anyway?"

"Veronica. He proposed to his first wife pretty quickly. They'd only known each other a month before tying the knot. Flynn believes if he hadn't married her, they would've imploded naturally, and way before an ugly divorce, or her cheating on him with his brother. A lot of pain could've been avoided."

"Garrett and Gwen had a quick engagement." Andy cast a worried glance in the direction of the tent. "Did Flynn and Veronica start out as happy as Garrett and Gwen?"

"No." That made her feel marginally better for her youngest sister. "Veronica and Flynn were never compatible where it counted."

"He and Sabrina seem to be on the same page."

"Those two." Gage emitted an amused sniff. "They've been best friends since college. Sabrina predated Reid and me by a few weeks. Somehow Sabrina and Flynn had circled each other for years. Too distracted by dating people other than each other, I guess."

"That's sweet." And it made sense. A relationship built over years and years had a strong foundation. "They seem solid. I can see why he didn't stick to his pact… But you did."

"Yes, the Brit and I carry that torch." A self-deprecating smile decorated Gage's handsome face. "For me it was about not being engaged again. For Reid, well, who the hell knows? He was in no matter what. He's never been one to get too attached."

"I know what that's like." When she found Gage regarding her with a curious head tilt, she explained. "It's hard to get attached and then be left behind. If you're not careful, your identity can become wrapped up in someone else."

"You're the independent sort."

"As are you."

He seesawed his head like he was turning over the

thought. "Not exactly. I'm a team player. I like having someone. I like dating but I rarely turn and burn them like Reid."

"You're a serial monogamist."

"I don't know about that. But I can definitely feel when I'm getting in too deep, or when she's getting in too deep, and that's when I button things up."

"Sounds sort of awful."

"You mean I sound awful now that you know how shallow I am?"

"No. I mean it sounds like an awful way to live. Like you're too afraid to keep going when there's potential for a real connection."

He watched her in silence for so long that a breeze swelled and she became aware of the music again. It also made her aware of the party they were missing.

The truth was she was afraid to pursue more with Gage, too. She'd never pursued deep connections in the past, even with her sisters. She'd gradually accepted that those sorts of relationships were for other people—people other than the Ice Queen, though that nickname had lost some of its sting.

She was changing, little by little, and the man next to her in the damp grass was a big reason why. She didn't know what that meant for them, but she did know that she wasn't giving him up just yet.

Outside of the "wedding bubble," and when they stopped pretending, did they have a prayer of making it last?

She wasn't sure that was the right question, considering Gage had made a pact never to marry anyone. She wasn't in the market for a husband, either, but she'd be lying if she said she'd never imagined what marriage might look like for her. How could she hang any hopes on what she and Gage had together, knowing that he'd walk away with hardly a second glance?

Since those thoughts were too big for her, and much too big for the end of a wedding reception, she shut them down.

"Come on." She stood and extended a palm to Gage, who was still sitting, his back to a particularly stout linden tree. "I need one more glass of champagne."

One more glass of champagne, one more dance and at least one more evening in Gage's arms before she lost her glass slipper at midnight.

Then it'd be airport, home, work and…whatever else followed. She hoped he still fancied her as much as he did in this moment.

Only time would tell.

Gregg and Lee Fleming had been residents of Leavenworth, Washington, for every year that Gage had been alive. The town was rich in Bavarian/German ancestry and boasted a festival every year to celebrate.

Gage's parents had been coworkers at the Leavenworth fish hatchery until recently, when his mother retired to start her own online business crafting quilts and pillows. His father still worked there and loved every moment of it, even though Gage had paid their mortgage off last year so that his father could retire. Stubborn old man.

Leavenworth was a shortish two-hour jaunt from Seattle, so Gage saw his parents often enough for his tastes.

His sister, Drew, admitted she'd like to see them a

little *less* often, but Gage had goaded her into hosting the family visit this time around.

Drew's apartment was in a nice, newish building in Seattle teeming with millennials and career-driven singles. She'd ended up as career-driven as Gage as it turned out, the worry of ending up at the hatchery a worst-case scenario for her as well.

"Mom is driving me crazy," Drew said in a harsh whisper as she pulled the lid off a pineapple upside-down cake their mother had brought for dessert.

Dinner had already been consumed—fish tacos, of course. Gage's father insisted on bringing his hard work to the table even though Gage had eaten enough fish to sustain him for a lifetime.

"I told her *three* times that Devin couldn't come to dinner because his schedule is too demanding and still she accuses me of 'hiding' him. I don't know why they want to meet him so badly anyway. He's a chef, not a celebrity."

Gage bit his lip. To Drew, chefs *were* celebrities. She was a public relations manager for various restaurants under the corporate umbrella of Fig & Truffle. She managed soft openings mostly and was a self-proclaimed foodie. She poked at the pineapple upside-down cake and frowned.

"I should've had Devin make crème brûlée."

"Don't be a snob."

She stuck her tongue out at him and he smiled. She left the room with a confidence that didn't used to be there. He admired the hell out of her for it—his sister hadn't always been so sure of herself.

She'd always been petite, though, which had been her downfall when she was younger. Her curvy figure had been named a "weight problem" by their less-than-eloquent mother, and Drew had referred to herself as "chubby" which showed even less eloquence.

Gage might have noticed his sister looked different at age sixteen versus age twenty, but it wasn't as if the fifty or so pounds she'd lost had made an iota of difference in how much he loved her.

He was glad she went after what she wanted. She'd always contended that good food was her number one passion, and she wouldn't sacrifice a pat of real butter for margarine no matter what health magazines suggested. She'd balanced her fitness goals and her passion, never indulging in too much of either one. Gage couldn't be prouder of his only sister.

He turned to resume making his and Drew's drinks, not the least bit intimidated by the fancy espresso maker in her apartment—they had one like it in the executive break room at Monarch. It made him laugh that while her dining room table was a scarred hand-me-down from their parents, her espresso maker was top-of-the-line and probably cost close to what it would take to replace that entire dining set twice over. Drew had her priorities straight, Gage thought with a smile.

Their parents had retired to the living room, which was connected to the kitchen. Drew came from that direction now to grab dessert plates as he finished their espressos.

He handed Drew one of the petite cups and she sagged against the countertop. "Why aren't they giving you a hard time about meeting who you're dating?"

"Because I never tell them I'm dating."

The TV was blaring so loudly that he was confident neither Mom nor Dad could overhear the discussion in the kitchen. Fine by him. The less they knew about his love life, the better.

"You would've been smart to keep Devin to yourself. Or Ronnie, for that matter," he said of her last bad breakup. Devin didn't have much more potential than Ronnie in that arena. Gage had met Devin once and, culinary degree aside, had determined he was a self-indulgent butthead, and that was putting it kindly.

"I *like* talking about my feelings." She sipped her espresso and her eyebrows jumped. "Mmm! This is delicious. So, big bro, do tell. Are you seeing anyone?"

He debated his answer for one sip, then two, from his espresso cup. Finally, he opted to level with Drew, since they'd been nothing but honest with each other for most of their lives. "Her name is Andy. I met her at work and she asked me to attend her sister's Ohio wedding with her last weekend as a favor."

As he spoke, his sister's eyebrows climbed her forehead until they were lost in her mahogany, previously mouse-brown hair. He hadn't gotten used to the darker hue yet.

"You went to a wedding in Ohio?"

"Yes."

"And then what?" She smiled like a loon.

"And then we came back to Seattle."

"Do you like her?"

"It'd be weird to attend a wedding with someone I didn't like, wouldn't it?"

"So coy. Where is she?"

"She's working."

"Monarch isn't open on Sunday."

"She works for herself. She was freelancing at Monarch." He and Drew had a mini standoff. "It's too soon to bring her in to meet the fam." *If ever.*

"I can't remember the last time you brought a girl around to 'meet the fam.'"

She was right. It hadn't been something he'd even considered. He couldn't say that he was considering it now, but when he'd mentioned to Andy he had a family thing today, he'd briefly entertained the idea of inviting her. He didn't, of course, because that would've been insane.

"What girl?" Their mother, Lee, strode into the kitchen.

Enter: the reason he hadn't invited Andy. His very loving, oft-prying mother.

"I want to hear all about her. Can you Face-Call her so we can meet her?"

"It's called FaceTime, Mom," Drew said.

"Face-Call, FaceTime. Whatever. Pull her up on your mobile phone so we can say hello."

Gage opened his mouth to say "hell, no," but their mother interrupted with "Do you have any real coffee, Drew darling? I don't like expresso."

Drew ignored their mother's mispronunciation of *espresso* and pulled a "real" coffee maker out of a lower cabinet. As she set up the drip pot, she smiled over her shoulder. "I don't think Gage is ready to introduce us to his girlfriend."

"She's not my girlfriend," he grumbled, sounding like a less mature version of himself.

"Well, why on earth not?" their mother asked.

"The same reason you won't introduce us to Devin? Are we that embarrassing?"

Gage grinned at his sister, content to have the topic swivel to her. "Yeah, Drew. Where *is* Devin tonight?"

"Working," she said between her teeth.

"Well, so is Andy."

"Oh! Her name is Andy! Isn't that darling?" Lee clapped her hands. "Tell me about her while Drew makes some real coffee."

Lee wrapped her arms around Gage's arm and dragged him out of the kitchen, peppering him with questions the whole way.

He couldn't be sure but he could swear he heard his sister's tinkling laughter follow him from the room.

Eighteen

The door to Flynn Parker's top-floor penthouse opened and Andy thought for a second she'd walked into a tomb. Gray walls, black floors and dark cabinetry greeted her from the kitchen, the room closest to the door. A few flickering jar candles on the surface further reinforced the "tomb" decor.

The feeling inside was nothing like a tomb, however, and neither were the people. Andy didn't typically hang out with a group of friends. She was a loner by nature, maybe in part due to her upbringing, and rarely spent this much time with anyone when the hours weren't being billed. Conversely, Gage had a strong network of friends, which was no surprise given his abundant charm.

She'd been working like a madwoman since they'd returned to Washington, but she'd made sure to allow time for Gage and his friends. She'd even sent a nice bottle of bourbon to him at the office. She was simply happy. And "simply" anything in a relationship had been an elusive beast until now.

"Andy!" Sabrina, dressed beautifully in a bright red knee-length dress, wore a smile that was both wide and infectious. "I'm so glad you could come. I wasn't sure if you would."

Honest as ever. Andy gave a demure smile, aware of Gage's palm warming her back. They'd been home for a little over a week now and things were surprisingly…good.

They'd been back to work, back to their own beds. Andy had seen Gage twice last week. Once for a late dinner that, thanks to a troublesome new client, had happened at 8:45 p.m., and once when she went to his apartment for what was supposed to be pizza and a movie and had ended up being pizza, half a movie and sex on the sofa.

"Well, you did corner her, love," Reid said, stepping into view to pour a glass of white wine, then turning to hand it to a blonde woman standing at his left elbow. "Kylie, this is Andrea Payne. Andy, Kylie Marker."

The blonde gave Andy a limp handshake and accepted her wine. "I like your…pants."

The compliment was forced, and so was Andy's smile. She'd worn simple black slacks and a pale blue silk shirt for work and hadn't had time to change. Kylie, on the other hand, looked like she'd been poured into her little black dress, her curvy form testing the seams. She was exactly the kind of woman Andy would expect to see Reid with, but somehow not… Reid's shrewd sense of humor and elegant wit seemed better suited for a woman who could match him blow for blow. Then again, according to Gage, Reid wasn't in the market for a challenge.

Anyway.

Andy had been near Monarch today, so she'd stopped by under the guise of "checking on the sales team" but in reality had wanted to see Gage. She'd been busy since she'd been home and was trying to fit him in when she could.

Missing someone was a new concept. She normally had her work to keep her warm at night. When Sabrina had poked her head into his office to invite him over to Flynn's penthouse for "Hump Day drinks," she'd swept her hand to include Andy in the invitation. Andy had automatically refused but Sabrina had instructed Gage to bring her with him.

Andy liked Sabrina. Liked all of them, truthfully. She hadn't expected to pull a lover out of offering to hire Gage as her fake boyfriend much less three new friends, but somehow she had.

"Red or white?" Gage asked her, helping himself to the line of wine bottles sitting on the countertop.

"White, please."

"That's what I have!" Kylie exclaimed with a grin. Reid arched one eyebrow like maybe he'd just now realized he'd settled for less than his equal.

"How about champagne?" Sabrina sent a saucy wink to Flynn, who was already moving for the fridge. She bounced over to the cabinet and began pulling out flutes to line up on the countertop.

"What's this, then?" Reid asked.

"An announcement of some sort, apparently."

Gage relinquished the wineglasses and stepped back, waiting while Flynn popped the cork off not one, but two bottles of Dom Pérignon.

"We're getting married!" Sabrina said as Flynn started pouring. She reached into her pocket and pulled out a shining diamond ring.

Whoa.

Andy suddenly felt out of place for an announcement this big.

The moment Sabrina slid the ring onto her finger, Kylie was on her like white on rice.

"It's beautiful." Kylie hugged Sabrina around the neck and Reid gently removed his date, who was now dabbing her eyes. "Sorry. I'm so moved when people get engaged. Or pregnant. Are you pregnant?"

"Um. No. But thanks for asking," Sabrina said with a wince.

Kylie shot a loving look up at Reid, and he turned the color of his sage-green tie. Yes, he'd recognized his shortsightedness when it came to Kylie. She was hearts and wedding bells and Reid wasn't looking for anything more than a good time.

"Congratulations, Sabrina. You two are good together and I'm happy for you." Andy accepted a champagne flute from Flynn. "Tell us how you asked."

Always a popular conversation starter in this situation.

"She was painting," Flynn said, his low baritone not hinting at what a softie he was on the inside. Andy had seen him around Sabrina at work. He virtually melted whenever she was near.

"He brought me a little paper sack from my favorite art store and when I pulled out the new paintbrush—" Sabrina couldn't finish, her throat clogging as tears came forth as easily as her smile.

"The ring was on the paintbrush. I said some stuff. The end." Flynn wrapped an arm around his fiancée and kissed her forehead while Sabrina swiped at her eyes.

Seriously. How sweet were they?

"Congrats, man," Gage said. Reid chimed in, too, lifting his flute and toasting their friends.

"Well, that was a surprise." Gage corralled Andy to one side, his hand on her back. Whenever he touched her, the stresses of the day vanished.

"A surprise? Even I could've guessed that was coming."

"I *suspected*. I wasn't sure."

"I like your friends. You're all sort of puzzling."

"Meaning?"

"Sabrina," Andy said, lowering her voice as they stepped farther into the apartment, "is so quirky you'd expect her to wear a peasant dress and flowers in her hair, but she favors fancy dresses. Flynn is gruff but it's for show, although this penthouse does make me question if he has a soul…or if he stores it in a trick wall somewhere in the penthouse."

Gage chuckled. "Sab's working on that. He inherited this place from his father. Emmons wasn't the warmest of men."

The painting over the mantel featured a pair of chickadees sitting side by side on a Japanese maple tree. The warm golds, blues and pinks were adorable and light and completely out of place in this house.

"I'm guessing that artistry was Sabrina's doing?"

"Definitely. Wait'll she moves in here. Her apartment is the equivalent of a peasant dress. Come on. I know you've got more to say." He made a give-it-to-me gesture.

"Okay. Reid is British class and pomp, the textbook playboy, but there's something about him that makes me wonder if he's acting. Though I'm not sure *he's* aware that he's acting."

"That's what every woman says about him. They've all tried to crack the Reid Code." They both looked at Kylie. "She's going to be disappointed when she doesn't succeed."

"Terribly. I can tell already she's not the one. Reid needs a woman who challenges him."

"To duels?"

"Challenges what he knows about himself." She gave Gage a playful shove.

"And what about me puzzles you, Andy?" He paired the question with his hands on her hips as he moved behind her to study the Seattle skyline out the window. In the background, his friends' laughter and banter continued.

"You were engaged before and made an unbreakable pact never to be married," she told Gage's reflection, "and yet you volunteered to come with me to a wedding and then didn't break things off after." She shrugged. "*Puzzling.*"

"I needed your expertise."

"Is that why I'm here right now?" Was she a version of Kylie? A temporary placeholder before he moved on to someone else?

"Andy."

"You like me more than anyone ever has, Gage." She spun in his arms and even though there was a time she would've died before doing something as casual as drape her arms on a man's shoulders within sight of a crowd, she did it anyway.

"Good." He placed a gentle kiss on her lips.

"Don't tell me you two are next," Reid said with a groan.

"Aw, but they're so cute!" Kylie chimed in.

Andy and Gage separated and she studied the floor for a beat. He had a way of making her forget where she was—who she was. Was she becoming one half of a whole? The idea of her being with anyone intrinsically was foreign, and after talking with Ness, frankly a little frightening.

"I know about the pact. He's safe," Andy said with a soft smile.

"Pact?" Kylie asked, her brow denting with a frown.

Ruh-roh.

Reid's nostrils flared. He sent Andy a withering glare and she mouthed the word *sorry.*

"Kylie, let's you and I step outside for a moment." Reid took a long look at the balcony and seemed to reconsider. "Actually, let's go out into the hallway. You'll catch a chill."

"In July?" Kylie asked as Reid hustled her out of the penthouse.

"I don't think he was comfortable telling Kylie about the pact with the prospect of a balcony and a long drop to the street," Gage said.

"Right." Andy's smile faded. "It's a strange pact for the three of you, considering your goals are so different."

"You didn't see Flynn when he was married." Gage shook his head.

"I didn't see you engaged to what's-her-face, either."

"She was a lot like you." This from Flynn, who strolled into his living room, his fiancée, and her million-watt smile, by his side. "Driven. Ambitious."

"But *not* like you," Sabrina offered, "in that she was about as warm as…"

"This penthouse?" Andy supplied.

"Exactly." Sabrina's smile was approving, her eyes narrow as she studied Gage. When her gaze snapped to Andy, it said *we'll talk later.*

Andy nodded. She was looking forward to learning more of Gage's secrets.

"Give it to me." Andy refilled Sabrina's flute in the kitchen.

Reid had returned from the hallway without Kylie. He told everyone that she'd left because she had an early morning tomorrow. No one believed him, but no one asked him to explain. Now the guys had vanished to parts unknown in the five-thousand-square-foot penthouse to shoot pool, while Sabrina and Andy lingered around the drinks and snacks.

"Give what to you?" Sabrina dragged a cucumber slice through the hummus and offered it. "This?"

"The way you were looking at Gage earlier, I could swear you came to some sort of conclusion."

Sabrina covered her smile by eating the cucumber slice, and then took a sip of her champagne before speaking.

"Gage and I have been friends for a long time. Almost as long as I've known Flynn. I've seen him date, and I remember Laura, although that was a long time ago. I know that he's charming, relaxed, a great date."

"He is all of those things," Andy said carefully.

"And yet with you—" Sabrina tilted her head "—he's serious, too. I can tell by the way he looks at you that he's not as light in his approach."

Uncomfortable and almost sorry she'd asked, Andy squirmed. "I'm fairly serious myself. I can see why he'd react accordingly."

Sabrina donned her best Mona Lisa smile before humming to herself.

"You're falling for him."

Andy coughed on her next sip of champagne. "What?" she croaked, trying to recover from inhaling her Dom.

Sabrina's knowing expression didn't change as she dragged a carrot through the hummus. "I can tell by the way you act around him. The way you look at him. Not in the same way Kylie looked at Reid, which was…*needy*."

Agreed.

"But like you're seeing a future without an end date."

"I'm in no danger of being proposed to by Gage," Andy sputtered. She was thrown by Sabrina's suggestion that she was "falling" for him. Thrown because she wasn't that well-versed in relationships. She was enjoying herself, that was all. But falling for him? Hmm…

"That dumb pact." Sabrina rolled her eyes. "They act like it's carved in stone. Then the right girl comes along and they learn it's more like chalk on a black-board."

That made sense for Sabrina and Flynn. They'd been friends since college—best friends. For Gage and Andy it was different. They'd known each other for what, a handful of weeks?

"You never know," was all Sabrina said.

But the lingering glance to her shining engagement ring told Andy everything she needed to know about what was going on in the brunette's mind.

Sabrina had changed Flynn's mind about the pact. If Andy and Gage were serious about having a future, could she change his mind, too?

Nineteen

"Where's Andrea tonight?" Reid lifted his beer and pegged Gage with a meaningful look. They sat side by side at the bar they usually haunted, though it was fairly dead for a Thursday night.

"Working."

Andy worked a lot. He'd had no idea how much he wouldn't see her when they returned to Seattle. But she was never too far away, either texting or visiting in between busy nights.

"Shouldn't you two be celebrating your three-week anniversary tonight?" Reid smirked.

"Very funny." Gage frowned.

"Refill?" Shelly, the bartender, gestured to Reid, whose glass was empty. The bar's overhead lights glinted off the ring on her finger, practically throwing sparks.

"That's new, love." Reid took her hand and turned the ring this way and that. "Are you spoken for?"

"I've *been* spoken for, but I suppose this makes it official. Bryan proposed this weekend." She beamed, her eyes sparkling like her new diamond ring.

That was a giant coincidence. Flynn had asked Sabrina this week. Love was in the air, Gage thought, shifting uncomfortably in his seat. He'd been flirting with Shelly the night he met Andy and he had no idea at the time that Shelly was someone else's.

Reid ordered two more beers and Gage tipped his draft back to drain the contents of his glass. Might as well have another.

"Soon I'll be the only keeper of the pact," Reid said with a melodramatic sigh.

"What's that supposed to mean?" Gage asked as Shelly delivered their beers and cleared away their empty mugs.

"Andy sent you an expensive bottle of liquor. To the office."

"It was a bottle of bourbon. Don't sound so foreboding."

"It means she was thinking about you. And then she unexpectedly dropped by before coming along with you to Flynn's." Reid's tone was conspiracy-theory low. "She's getting comfortable, mate. *Girlfriendy.*"

"What are you talking about?" Gage laughed to dismiss the whole "girlfriendy" thing, but he had to admit she sort of was and it wasn't bothering him as much as it should.

"With anyone else you'd be letting her down gently. But you haven't yet, have you?"

"Not yet." The words settled into the pit of Gage's stomach. He wasn't sure why. He'd been the one to suggest they keep seeing each other after Andy's sister's wedding. He'd been the one to insist on her coming to Flynn's that night. *Where another engagement was announced*, he thought nervously as he caught the glint off Shelly's ring.

"Keeper of the pact," Reid announced, lifting his beer again.

Reid was being ridiculous. Gage was no closer to proposing to Andy than he was to climbing on top of this bar and stripping.

And yet…

Something had been welling up inside him. An uncomfortable…what was the word? *Rightness*.

He felt *right* with Andy and he hadn't had that feeling in a long, long time. And never this soon. Even with Laura, he'd been acting more on expectations than emotion.

Why was that?

"It's in the air," Reid said, echoing Gage's earlier thought. He sneered. "Love. You've not caught it, have you?"

"Love?" Gage laughed. "No. Definitely not."

If love was like an airborne virus, he could write off that weird pit-of-his-gut feeling to proximity. He'd been at a weekend wedding with Andy where every event dripped with romance. And now two of his closest friends were engaged to be married. Romance tended to be like glitter. It stuck to you, undetected unless the light hit it just right, and almost impossible to get rid of once you noticed it.

Was Andy like glitter?

Yes. And no.

She wasn't annoying or clingy. She wasn't staying at his place or leaving her stuff there. She was good on her own and didn't need his reassurance. But she was different than she'd been when they first met. She was independent but including him in her life.

Like he'd asked. Because he'd caught the airborne glitter virus and was infected. He swiped at his sweaty brow.

Possibly he was freaking out.

"It's not too late," his British friend warned, his tone scarily serious. "You've been down this road with plenty of women. If it's time to insert some distance, you know how to do it. Is it time?"

Gage let out a choking sound. "You make it sound like there's a lot of them. I date less than you do."

Deflection was the best tactic whenever backed into a corner.

"I date because I'm great at it. You date because you like being part of a couple."

Gage blinked at his friend. He liked having company, yes, but the "part of a couple" accusation wasn't true.

Was it?

Andy had accused him of being a serial monogamist. He wasn't like Reid, showing up with a new girl at every event, but neither was he Flynn and Sabrina, attached at the hip. Gage was somewhere in the middle. A "gray area" when it came to women in general and relationships at large.

"You're quite good at having girlfriends. Women like you so bloody much."

"They're not girlfriends." Aware he sounded like

a twelve-year-old, Gage stopped slumping and sat straighter on his stool.

Reid smirked. "Well, they're different from hook-ups, which is what I'm best at."

"You're bragging about being forgettable, Reid."

"Not forgettable. Just...*unkeepable*." He nodded, happy with his own conclusion.

Gage had sworn to uphold the pact in part for Flynn, but also for himself. After his engagement imploded and Laura left, Gage never wanted to feel that unmoored again.

Success was important to him in all things. In school, he'd graduated with a 4.0 GPA—even though it meant working harder to lift his suffering grades. When he dated Laura and determined she was as ambitious as he was, it was a perfect match. He'd *known* she was The One.

Until he didn't.

Laura had come at him with a whopper of an announcement just one month after announcing their engagement. He wasn't good enough for her. Wasn't as successful as she wanted him to be. Worse, she said he never would be. *"You don't want to be in a partnership where your wife is earning more than you, Gage."*

It rankled him that she thought he'd care about how much money she earned, and how it compared to his salary. That he'd be that shallow. And then it rankled him all over again that she'd basically hobbled him, telling him he couldn't be as successful as her, when she knew damn well that success and Gage went hand in hand.

Nothing he'd said to that effect had changed Laura's

mind. Her mind was made up when she'd invited him to that diner for lunch. She'd set the stage for a public breakup, and had pulled out an actual bullet-pointed list. She'd read from the notebook, never stopping to look at him.

On the surface they'd seemed like a good match, but Laura found him too "casual" and not serious enough for her taste. "We're too different," she'd told him. He'd learned that day that she was right about that. Gage was a human being with real feelings and a heart, while Laura was a cyborg with faulty programming.

It was the biggest failure of his life, that relationship—the engagement that never produced a wedding. He'd been certain of a future with Laura. One that stood the test of time like his parents' marriage. Being that wrong had thrown him. It wasn't any wonder he'd leaped into the pact the way he did…twice.

Failure in business happened, of course. He wasn't so delusional he thought himself impervious to stepping in it now and again. But failing with relationships was trickier to pull out of. His grades had temporarily dipped when Laura and he split. His social life exploded, and he'd chosen to go to parties instead of study. Hookups were a tack he tried and failed at. He didn't like meaningless flings. And yet he didn't want to be roped in again by a woman who promised forever and backed out before giving him a chance to be a success.

Laura thought they were too different? Fine. He'd date fun-loving women who valued him for who he was. He'd back out before it became too much for either of them. It was hard at first, learning how to let them down easy and walk away whole, but he'd been successful at that, too.

Then came Andy.

Independent, driven, successful Andy.

Vulnerable, open, *fascinating* Andy.

The idea of them splitting sent his mind reeling. Made his stomach toss. He'd suggested they not end things and she trusted him. He cared about her and didn't want her hurt. Would she carry his rejection with her like a wound? Or would she harness her driven, independent side and soar without him?

Option B was the *only* option. He couldn't even think about leaving a scar as deep as Matthew Higgins and his "Ice Queen" comments. Andy was better than that.

But she was also better than sticking around with a guy who wouldn't give her what she ultimately deserved.

Forever.

He'd seen the way she looked at her sister, Gwen, at the wedding. Andy might not be able to admit it to herself yet, but Gage could tell she was a woman who wanted to be married someday. And he couldn't—*wouldn't*—allow himself to take those vows.

A sigh came from the depths. He knew what he had to do. He couldn't let Andy settle for less than she deserved any more than he could string her along. Their relationship would end eventually. And maybe if he ended it sooner it'd save them both a lot of heartache.

His chest seized at the thought of not seeing her or holding her again. Of not kissing her ever again. He'd miss her like hell. He already felt like part of him was tangled up in part of her. He couldn't let his unreliable heart call the shots, though, arguably, he'd already let it call a few.

No part of this was going to be easy. He already cared about Andy ten times, hell, *one hundred times*, more than he'd cared about Laura. And he'd been *in love* with Laura.

Or so he'd thought.

It was possible, even probable, that he'd been fooled into thinking what he was feeling for Andy was deep, unfathomed and long-lasting. As if he'd been glamoured by the couples-in-love around him and had acted on what he thought was instinct but was more…conditioning.

And if he didn't proceed very carefully, Andy could fall into the same trap.

At his elbow, Gage's phone buzzed with a text message from her.

I have dinner for us. It's Thai. Your place or mine?

Gage's chest tightened when he thought of Andy's bright eyes and strawberry-blond hair. When he thought of what he had to do he knew he had to do it before either or both of them said or did things that were unable to be taken back.

He realized now that he'd made a mistake not ending this after the wedding. He wasn't too big of a man to admit he was wrong, even if he had let things go on for far too long. Andy deserved that same respect.

My place, he texted back.

His home turf would be better. Then she could storm out like he guessed she would. Drive to a girlfriend's house and curse his name a thousand times over. There was no time like the present to recover from the misstep—before she expected more than he'd be able to give. Before she got in any deeper, or he gave her any *wronger* of an impression about himself.

He pulled money out of his wallet to pay and Reid's eyebrows rose. "Duty calls? Or should I say booty calls?"

Gage was so miserable he couldn't crack even the smallest of smiles. "You're not in the pact alone, Reid."

"No?"

"No." Gage shoved his untouched beer in front of Reid and nodded. "I know what I need to do."

He'd been pretending, which was fun at first, but now it'd gone too far. It was time to wrap up this farce with Andy.

Past time.

Twenty

Andy had never been so cheery. Happy, sure. Contented, absolutely. But joyful, humming a tune as she strolled into the high-rise holding Gage's posh apartment? She couldn't remember ever feeling this buoyant.

She hadn't been very good at balancing her time at work and her time with Gage. Tonight she was going to make it up to him. She was ambitious and she was driven and, frankly, didn't have a lot of experience including another person in her plans.

Andy wanted to include Gage for one simple reason: she loved him.

She was certain of it.

She'd been ordering shrimp pad thai and basil fried rice and it hit her as she paid for their dinner.

For the first time in a long time, she was half of a whole.

As unexpected as it was, and in such a short period of time, she'd fallen in love with Gage Fleming. She hadn't seen it coming but now that it was here, she welcomed it. As much as she contended that she didn't need anyone, she needed him. And what's more was that she didn't mind needing him. It didn't make her feel weaker or less independent. She felt stronger for it.

Love.

She finally was beginning to understand what all the fuss was about.

Excited about her newfound discovery, she'd grinned at the cashier and said, "My boyfriend and I are having dinner together."

The cashier smiled quizzically but wished her well, having no idea the monumental shift that had occurred in the ten minutes Andy sat in the restaurant and waited for her takeout.

Falling in love *was* monumental. And even though it was after nine o'clock, and even though the food was greasy Thai instead of a five-star meal, Andy was certain of her feelings for Gage.

She couldn't wait another second to tell him how he'd changed her. There'd even been a stray thought about how they could tell their grandkids one day about how they'd met. The bar story. It would kill!

Humming and happy, she pushed the number eighteen button in the elevator and rode to Gage's floor. She'd tell him tonight. He deserved to feel as great and whole and happy as she did.

She stepped out and admired her surroundings. The building Gage lived in was historical, with charming woodwork and brass handles on the doors.

The lighting fixtures appeared original to the building, though Andy guessed they'd been rewired. Everything functioned and felt modern while at the same time throwing her back several decades. It was remarkable the way history worked. She was making some for Gage and herself tonight.

His apartment door was cracked, the soothing notes of jazz coming from inside. Andy knocked lightly before letting herself in. The entryway opened to a wide living room with a wall of windows letting in the moonlight. The couch was navy with deep red pillows, which had reminded her of Gwen's wedding colors the first time Andy had been here.

It was a sign. She never would've thought that before tonight, but being in love had given her new vision. Who knew what a superpower that could be?

Gage stood in the kitchen beyond the living room, pouring wine into two glasses. Red.

The color of love.

Andy was so excited she was about to burst.

"Your dinner, sir." She set down the paper sack and sidled over to kiss him. He delivered a kiss but his lips were firm and pursed, his brow a furrowed thundercloud.

"You okay?" she asked.

She lifted her wineglass and took a sip, wondering what it was that had turned Gage's mood sour. Work, most likely.

"You go first," she told him. "I had a not-so-great day at the office, too. I'll commiserate with you."

Her smile faded as a look of hurt crossed his features.

"Andy." The way he said her name was ominous. A premonition of something horrible.

The food that had once smelled tantalizing and tempting now caused her stomach to flop like a dying fish.

"I've never lied to you before and I have no intention of starting now."

"Oh?" Her hand shook, and her wineglass with it.

He pulled in a deep breath, paused to drink down half the contents of his glass and then faced her. He put the glass down. Then warm hands braced her biceps and a million alarms rang out in her head.

In a panic, she blurted, "I love you. I realized when I was picking up your shrimp pad thai that we belong together. What we have, this isn't impermanent. This is the real thing. I know it's fast and I know you have that pact, but Flynn ditched the pact for Sabrina. Do you know why?"

Gage's expression teetered on mortified, but for Andy her dam had broken. She couldn't stop talking now that she'd started.

"Flynn realized that being in love with Sabrina was more important than some silly pact," she continued. "Sabrina was someone worth making new decisions for. Flynn wanted to move forward with her because he'd seen a part of her he'd never seen before. *Gage.* That's you and me." She didn't dare slow down until she said the rest. "You were the one who excavated that part of me. I didn't know how to be half of a couple. I didn't know how to be in love. You were the one who opened those doors—who taught me how to love you."

Her voice broke. She swallowed thickly and waited.

She'd said what she'd come here to say, and as na-
ively as a virgin bride on her wedding night, she expected him to have come to the same realization as
she had. She hadn't even considered that he didn't feel
the same way. How could he not?

She saw now that she'd been dead wrong. The evidence was written all over his stricken face.

"Say something." Her voice was a broken whisper, her heart threatening to break right alongside it.

"We went to a wedding together," he said. Bi-
zarrely.

"Yes." She let loose a shaky smile.

"And then Flynn and Sabrina announced their engagement. Shelly's engaged, too, by the way."

"Who?"

"Bartender at From Afar."

"Oh." She wasn't following.

"I was engaged, Andy. And Laura ended that engagement because she didn't believe in us. She was
cold and calculated and completely dismissive of who
we could've become."

"I'm not." Andy gripped his hands, trying to head
off another argument before it brewed. "I'm forever
material. I'm a single Payne sister—the last of my kind.
You opened my eyes to the fact that I'm valued and
worth it. You opened my eyes to a life outside of my
business. You opened my eyes to love."

"I can't love you, Andy. I can't let this go on any
longer." His voice was hard and tight, like the words
were fighting being spoken. "It's irresponsible."

"You…*can't*?"

"No."

Such a final word. She dropped his hands and he backed away from her a step.

Backed.

Away.

"You weren't supposed to fall in love with me, Andy. Hell, I'm not sure you are in love with me. You were caught up in your sister's romantic getaway, and I'm sure Sabrina said something last night that made you think you were—and that's not your fault. She's in love. Completely smitten. She thinks everyone can have what she and Flynn have."

For as gobsmacked as she felt, Gage might as well have reached out and slapped her.

"You think I don't know if I'm in love with you?" Gage was *deep* in the danger zone and hopefully her tone was conveying that fact. "You think I was swept up in wedding bells and engagement rings rather than coming to the conclusion about my feelings on my own?"

"Yes—" his voice rose incrementally "—I do. So was I. Too caught up to recognize we were both flirting with disaster. I'm not too big a man to admit I'm sorry."

"You're *sorry*?" she snapped.

"I never should've asked for more when I knew damn well I couldn't be the guy to give you more. Staying together is setting us up for a huge fall. A huge *failure*. I won't keep you from your future husband and waste any more of your time. What we had at Gwen's wedding was a perfect weekend. I should've left it at that."

Her hand twitched at her side. She'd never wanted to slap someone before. She did now. Just so he could feel the way she felt—like her stable footing had crumbled beneath her and she was in a free fall toward the cold, hard ground.

She settled for lifting her glass and throwing her remaining wine at him. Unaccustomed to being physically reactive, she sort of chickened out at the end and the splash fell short of his chest, landing on one side of his crisp white button-down shirt. Right about where the coffee stain was the day he'd talked her into letting him be her pretend boyfriend.

God. She'd never been so stupid.

"Bastard." Tears threatened but she swallowed down her rioting emotions.

"I'm sorry."

"The sorriest," she agreed. "Enjoy your meal."

She stomped out of his apartment without looking back, rode the elevator to the ground floor and marched to her car parked on the curb. She'd congratulated herself when she'd parked there, thinking how "lucky" she'd been to find the coveted space.

Lucky and in love.

"I'm *so* stupid," she reiterated aloud as she turned the key in the ignition. She'd known in her heart of hearts that forever wasn't for her. She'd let that doubt go, trusting Gage so implicitly that she'd agreed when he suggested they keep seeing each other. She'd allowed herself to believe the future was an open expanse with wildflowers blooming and horses galloping…

A fantasy.

One she wouldn't let herself wallow in no matter what her stupid heart thought. She could be in love with him all she wanted, but it didn't mean she couldn't move on. Gage might've put the final nail in the "them" coffin, but she had the power not to allow him in ever again.

Maybe someday she'd find it in her heart to be grateful to him for teaching her how to open up and trust and love someone.

Today was not that day.

She drove home without a backward glance, lecturing her tear ducts most of the way. The moment she twisted the lock on her front door and she was safely ensconced inside her own dark apartment, those tears came anyway, and showed no signs of stopping.

Gage stuffed his soiled shirt into the trash can hidden beneath the sink and washed Andy's wineglass, standing it on end in the dish drainer.

Then he moved to the kitchen counter, palmed the back of his neck and eyed the untouched bag of food with the receipt stapled to the paper bag.

He'd done the right thing.

But he still felt awful about it.

He finished his wine, surmising that Andy might never forgive him, but she could be free now. That he could continue working and upholding the pact because he believed wholeheartedly that engagement and marriage weren't for him. That his "feelings" couldn't be trusted because everyone in his vicinity was drunk on love.

It sounded like bullshit, even to him, so he couldn't imagine how badly it'd sounded when Andy was standing in his kitchen dumping her heart out.

What he'd done was the equivalent of stabbing her in the center of that heart with a dull knife.

"She'll get over it."

She'd have to. *He'd* have to. Viruses had to run their course, and the one he'd caught from her was a doozy. The "L" virus. He couldn't so much as think the four-letter word that hovered in the room like the scent of Thai food. His stomach gave an insistent rumble.

"Screw it." He tore open the bag, pulled out his shrimp pad thai and stowed the other container in the fridge for later.

Things didn't work out, that's all. And if the only carnage left behind from their breakup was a bag of Thai food, well, then they'd escaped relatively unscathed.

But as he dug his fork into his dinner and chewed forlornly, he questioned if he'd escaped unscathed after all.

The flavor should've burst—the shrimp was utter perfection, and the seasoning on point. Instead it was as if he was navigating a mouthful of foam packing peanuts.

"Virus," he said around another big bite. Viruses changed the flavor of food and altered a person's physical being. Which also explained that ache in the center of his shirtless chest.

He didn't hear any loud, blaring alarms like he had early on with Andy. There was only a low hum after the fallout. The sense that the worst wasn't coming, but had already come and gone. The sense that he'd made a giant mistake—one he could never take back.

He carried his dinner and wine to the couch where his heavy limbs dragged him down. Then he turned on the television and zoned out.

This, too, would pass.

Twenty-One

Gage looked up from his keyboard. Yasmine was typing away on her own laptop, and behind her Flynn's office was dark. Sabrina's, too. Flynn and Sabrina had left earlier. Something about meeting with a wedding planner and the only time the woman had available was three o'clock today.

When Gage glanced in the direction of Reid's office, he found his British friend wasn't in his chair, but heading Gage's way, whistling.

What the hell is he so happy about?

"Gagey, Gagey, Gagey." Reid said as he entered Gage's office.

"What?"

"Let's bugger off and grab drinks at Afar. It's dead in here. Everyone else has gone." He gestured to the empty-save-for-Yasmine floor.

"Pass." Gage returned his attention to the computer screen, where literally nothing was happening. He'd opened a blank document to type up a progress report for Flynn…that wasn't due for another month. He'd been spending a lot of hours in the office since he had nothing better to do than pass the time alone in his apartment.

The past nine and a half days had been absolute torture.

The feelings he'd convinced himself were fleeting and temporary hadn't gone anywhere. He'd given himself a week to recover from breaking things off with Andy, even though his instincts were bucking like a wild bronco. Everything about her leaving his apartment had felt wrong. Three days, five days— hell, nine and a half days later, it still felt wrong.

"You need to talk to someone and I'm offering my ear. But I'd rather do it over a beer." Reid unbuttoned his suit jacket and sat in the stuffed chair next to a plant.

"You and I talked already."

"I'm your best friend."

"You *were*."

Reid ignored the jab, pulling a hand over his face and muttering a swear word into his palm. "I tried to tell you."

Since Gage held Reid mostly responsible for leading him to think he needed to end things with Andy, that arrogant "I tried to tell you" comment sent his anger through the roof. He spun the chair to face his "friend."

"What, exactly, did you try to tell me, Reid?"

"That you had a girlfriend. That you liked being

part of a couple. That I, alone, would hold true to the pact." He put a fist to his heart like a knight taking an oath.

"I seem to remember you telling me that it was past time to let her down gently."

"I never said that. I said I expected you to have let her down gently by then."

Gage's frown intensified; he could literally feel an ache forming between his eyebrows. "You planted a seed of doubt."

"You've got a whole garden of doubt in there on your own. Don't pin this on me. I don't want to see you hurt any more than you do, but I'm under no delusions when it comes to who I am and what I want. You, on the other hand…"

Reid shrugged and Gage wanted to hit his friend's perfectly square jaw. Or hit *someone*. At the moment hitting *himself* was justified.

"That night we went to From Afar," Gage started. "I broke up with Andy under your advice." When Reid opened his mouth to argue, Gage added, "Encouragement. Whatever. You weren't rooting for us, so don't pretend you were."

Reid's turn to frown. Good. Gage liked watching his friend's smug face slip into an expression that was borderline apologetic.

"I love her, Reid." Gage said it like he was announcing that he had only days to live. That was what that epiphany felt like.

He loved Andrea Payne and she hated him.

"Does she love you?"

Gage's heart suffered another fissure, but he barely felt it. He'd been in so much pain over the last week-plus he'd gotten used to it. "She loved me nine and a half days ago."

"Love." Reid's tone was as grave as Gage's. "It is soon."

"I don't need your commentary. You've helped enough already."

He stood and Reid did, too, stepping in front of Gage to block the path to the door.

Reid put his hand on Gage's chest to keep him from walking out. "You can't blame me for this. I was being myself. Doing what I've always done. Which is bust your bollocks. It was your job to tell me to shove it. To stand up for what you and Andy had if it was so bloody important."

Gage's shoulders sagged. "You're right."

His buddy was right.

Andy had been right.

"Andy mentioned that Flynn had thrown aside the pact because Sabrina was worth it. He was able to see it. We all were. But that was Sab." Someone who'd been in Flynn's life for a long time, not a brand-new relationship with a vulnerable, gorgeous, cautious redhead.

"First," Reid started. "Sab is a unicorn. When it came to him tossing aside the pact, we never would've stood for it had it been the wrong woman. Second, you're wrong about Flynn being the white knight. He had his head up his arse until you and I dragged him to the conclusion that he'd always belonged to Sabrina."

Gage blinked. Damn. He'd forgotten that day in Flynn's office, where Reid and Gage had to have a "come to Jesus" talk with their third musketeer.

"Points to you for realizing you're in love with Andy before Flynn and I had to come in here and pull it out of you as well." Reid patted Gage's chest and dropped his arm to his side.

"Doesn't matter. I'm too late."

Reid's mouth pressed into a line.

"Andy vanished. She's back to being the unreachable Andy Payne. She's a puff of smoke. I tried her assistant after Andy ignored a few of my calls." Gage shook his head. "Nothing."

"Did you text her?"

Gage nodded. He couldn't lay his love for her out in writing and watch it be ignored, so he'd settled for one We need to talk and a follow-up At least let me apologize.

Unsurprisingly, she hadn't responded.

He understood her caution. She'd come to him, her bright blue eyes shining with happiness, and told him to his face that she was in love with him. She deserved the same from him and he'd been too chickenshit to admit as much. Then he'd broken up with her, telling her he was sorry. *Sorry.* Like an apology would undo the hurt.

He'd never regret anything like he regretted letting her walk out of his apartment that night.

"Not like you don't know where she lives," Reid offered.

"I don't, actually. We always met at restaurants, or the airport, or she'd come to my place after she was done with work. She's impossible to track down."

"Nothing's impossible." Reid's eyes twinkled knowingly.

But it was too late. Andy had moved on. And really, wasn't it fair to *let her* move on? To let her go and heal when he'd wadded up her love for him and thrown it in her face?

"This came for you." Yasmine interrupted them before Gage could share his thoughts. She handed him an envelope and he blinked at it stupidly. "I'm done for the day, unless either of you need me?"

"Take care, Yasmine. We're heading out soon ourselves," Reid told her.

She grabbed her purse and left while Gage stood frozen in the doorway of his own office.

"What is it, then?" Reid asked.

Gage showed Reid the envelope. The printed return address in professional block lettering read *Andy Payne, LLC* followed by a PO Box number.

Monarch had paid the invoice for her services upon her arrival, so what was it? Gage half expected it to be a letter saying, "You're a dick," or maybe another invoice with a line item for "breaking my heart" with a dollar amount next to it. Two thousand dollars, maybe.

He tore open the envelope and pulled out the single item within. A check.

His guess wasn't far off. But instead of being billed, he was being paid.

His eyes locked onto the words *Pay to the order of* and then snapped to the dollar amount—$2,000.00.

She'd written him a check for two thousand dollars.

On the memo line it read *Payment in full for business trip.*

There was nothing else in the envelope. No note. No "Fuck you." It was no less than he deserved—a final middle finger for what had happened in his apartment nearly ten days ago.

Reid let out a long, low whistle. "Harsh."

Then Gage arrived at a conclusion that hit him as hard and fast as a shot. "Except it's not."

"No?"

"No." If Andy was mad at him, she *never* would've sent him this check. What better retaliation was there than freezing him out and never speaking to him again? Instead she'd *reached out*. She might even be as brokenhearted as he was, which could mean she still loved him. Receiving this check meant she cared. About him. About *them*.

She wasn't an Ice Queen.

They both knew it.

Gage's smile found his face without him trying. "She loves me. Still."

"You're insane. That's a cold move."

"I know what it looks like, but trust me when I tell you that this—" he waved the check "—means she's not over us yet." He knew it in his heart. A heart that he'd have to serve up on a platter if he had a prayer of earning her back. "I have to tell her that I love her, too. Right now. And in person. Can you find her?"

Reid's mouth flinched into a grimace briefly— likely at the prognosis of his friend falling in love. Couldn't be helped. Gage loved Andy, and distance and time hadn't done anything to dampen that love. In fact, his feelings for her had only intensified.

"Please."

With a sigh, Reid announced, "I'm a computer-hacker-turned-IT-wizard. Of course I can find her."

He tilted his head toward his office, where no fewer than three large computer screens decorated his desk. "Tell me everything you know about the mysterious Andy Payne."

Twenty-Two

Andy reread the email to her webmaster for the third time, a zing of excitement and nervousness comingling in her belly. It was past time she came out of hiding and let the world, or at least the world wide web, see her for who she truly was.

Mike, attached you'll find my headshot. Please update the website to include my photo and an About page. My bio is below. If you have any questions, let me know.

She'd never had the confidence before to stand on her own merits. She'd made many, many excuses about why she needed to keep her identity a secret from her clients, but since the breakup with Gage she'd taken a long, hard look at her life. She was done hiding. Done trying to live up to the tough-as-nails woman she'd created as a persona. She'd thought it would protect her, but instead she only felt like a coward for hiding behind that persona. It was time to step into her power. A power, ironically, that she wouldn't have if it wasn't for Gage.

He'd undone her completely. He'd peeled back layer after layer and had seen her in her most vulnerable state. He'd wooed her from her shell and defended her honor and made her realize that above all else, she was enough.

Exactly as she was.

She closed her eyes and willed back the torrent of emotions that had plagued her since the night they broke up. She couldn't change what had happened any more than she could keep from still loving him.

He'd texted. He'd called. She'd ignored both, knowing she couldn't face him with her tender underbelly showing. She had been desperately trying to rebuild her armor, to rebrick the wall that she'd been hidden safely behind that evening at the bar, when she'd offered Gage two grand in exchange for his accompaniment to Gwen's wedding.

Hiding had proved impossible.

Gage hadn't only lured her out from behind that wall, but he'd also demolished the way she'd seen the world prior to him.

Andy knew she was desirable and, unlike Gage, she wasn't afraid to face her future.

That didn't mean her heart didn't ache, or that she didn't soak her pillow every night with fresh tears, but it did mean that she wasn't the Ice Queen Matthew had accused her of being. She was a feeling, sensitive, vulnerable woman. Beautifully vulnerable.

Being vulnerable sucked.

She sent the email and shut her laptop, mind on the bottle of white wine chilling in the door of the fridge. It was ten thirty and her eyes were heavy, drooping from the fatigue of both work and personal matters.

Wine would help.

Before she'd taken her first sip of crisp, light pinot grigio, her cell phone rang. The jingle made her heart leap to her throat even though she'd silenced Gage's phone number days ago. She couldn't bring herself to delete his phone number yet. Soon, though, she'd have to close the door on what they had.

The screen showed Vanessa's photo, and Andy took a steeling breath. Rare was the occasion Ness called her, and the news was rarely good.

"Ness, hi."

"Is it too late to call?"

"No. Just wrapped up work, actually. I poured a glass of wine and was about to have my first sip."

"I'll join you. I have a bottle open." There was the sound of a cabinet opening and closing, liquid pouring. "Cheers, sis."

Andy joined her in a cross-country sip and waited for Ness to say why she'd called. She didn't have to wait long.

"Alec and I are separating. Separated. Past tense. He moved out this afternoon."

"Ness." Andy's heart, which was already crushed, hurt for her sister. "I'm so sorry."

"I wanted to tell you personally. A divorce is probably on the horizon, but we're trying living apart to see how things go."

Andy guessed that could go one of two ways. Either absence would make the heart grow fonder, or that other adage—out of sight, out of mind—would make them forget why they'd ever liked each other.

For Andy, it was option A. She wanted to believe that Gage reaching out meant that he felt the same way, but there was no way to be sure unless she contacted him. She hadn't been brave enough to do that—and quite possibly never would be brave enough.

"How's life?" Ness asked. Caught off guard by her sister's conversational tone, Andy surprised herself by answering honestly.

"Horrible. Gage and I..." She swallowed down a lump of sadness. "We broke up."

Ness let out a cynical laugh. "You should consider yourself lucky you didn't invest years in him before things went downhill. What I'm going through isn't for the faint of heart."

An insensitive comment was completely expected from her sister, but Andy didn't clam up like she used to. The new Andrea Payne didn't make herself smaller to avoid hurt feelings. She stood up for herself.

"You know you're not the only one with problems, Vanessa," Andy snapped. "Your pain doesn't eclipse mine or make what I'm going through any less upsetting. I'm a human being with feelings, not the Ice Queen whose heart is frozen into a solid block. I was in love with him. *Am* in love with him."

"Andy—"

"I told him," Andy continued, her voice watery. "I

told him I loved him, because while I might not be the Ice Queen, I am very, very stupid. I laid everything on the line even though he told me from the beginning he didn't want to be married. Why didn't I listen?"

Her mini rant ended with tears slipping down her cheeks. She went to the couch, wineglass forgotten. It wouldn't help her to drink it.

Nothing would help her but time.

"Sweetheart." Ness sounded almost motherly, definitely sisterly. The hard edge from her voice was gone. "You are not stupid. You're the smartest of all of us. If there was a mistake made, it wasn't you falling in love, it was that Gage was too blind to see what he had. He really missed out on an incredible life with you."

The tears dried on Andy's cheeks as she held the phone gently against her ear. "Thanks."

"What a jackwagon."

Andy surprised herself by laughing at her sister's choice of name-calling. Even Ness let out a little chuckle.

"I have a way of letting my own misery overflow onto others," Ness said. "I'm bossy and rude. I want what's best for you, but somehow it comes out like I'm judgmental. No wonder Alec is leaving me."

"Stop talking about my sister that way."

Ness let out another laugh.

"Are you and Alec going to counseling?"

"He asked me if I would." A pause. "I told him I'd think about it."

"Ness, don't let your pride ruin what you and Alec have. I can't pretend to know what it's like to be married as long as you have, but I've seen you two together. You're good for each other. You were at some point, anyway. Is it unfixable?"

"I want to believe it's fixable but I'm afraid to try." Ness's voice trembled. "I don't ever want to feel this way again. I wonder if it'd be easier to make a rule to never get this close to someone rather than to try again and fail."

A rule...or a pact.

Andy thought of Gage and wondered for the first time since he dumped her if she wasn't the braver of the two of them. She was the one who faced her fears and won—he'd faced them and retreated.

"Don't make a rule," Andy told her sister. "Don't rob yourself of something great—whether it's Alec or a man in your future you overlook because you were hurt once before. Don't let the pain you're feeling now keep away the joy you could have later."

"See?" Vanessa sniffled, but there was a smile in her voice. "I told you that you were the smartest one."

They chatted for another twenty minutes, until Andy's eyes grew heavy and Ness begged off. She promised to call Alec and schedule the counselor, and thanked Andy for her help.

They exchanged I-love-yous, another rarity between them, and Andy curled up on the couch and closed her eyes, contented at least in part that she'd helped Ness through a rough evening.

Andy woke up to the insistent buzz-buzz-buzz of her phone. She cracked open one eye and checked the screen. It was her apartment's front desk, and typically they called only when there was a visitor or a delivery.

She blinked, her bleary eyes fighting to focus on the clock on the wall. Midnight wasn't prime visiting or delivery hours.

"Hello?" Her voice was groggy and sleepy, her mind not doing a very good job of understanding what the woman who called was saying to her.

But Andy made out two pertinent bits of information.

Gage Fleming was in the lobby.

And he wanted to come up and see her.

"He said it's urgent, Ms. Payne."

She had no idea how Gage had found her address. She hadn't purposely kept it from him—it'd been easier to meet him on her way home from work or at the airport when they'd flown to Ohio—but she was grateful he didn't know where to find her when her wounds were so fresh.

That he'd found her at all meant one of two things. A) He was angry about the check she'd sent and wanted to throw it in her face; or B) He wanted to explain himself since he hadn't shown an iota of tact when he'd broken up with her a week and a half ago.

Not that there was any great way to tell someone you didn't love them.

"Send him up." She'd hear what he had to say. She was brave. Strong. And unafraid.

How much more could he hurt her after he'd tossed her heart into the dirt?

After a quick check in the mirror by the front door to make sure her mascara wasn't on her cheeks— it wasn't—Andy opened the door and waited in the doorway with her arms folded.

She unfolded her arms and straightened, unsure

if she wanted him to see her in a defensive position. Then folded them again anyway.

Dammit.

She was nervous.

Even though she wanted with all her heart not to be.

But you don't have all of your heart, do you?

No. The man currently riding the elevator up to her apartment had at least 30 percent of it.

Maybe forty.

She refused to give him more. Not without him reciprocating.

From her front door she had a vantage point of the elevator, so she watched when Gage stepped from it. He was still in his office clothes, a pale blue pin-striped shirt and trousers, a navy tie knotted at his neck. In one hand was an envelope.

She froze when he spotted her. His mouth was un-smiling and his gait long and strong. As he strode to-ward her she had no idea if he'd chosen A or B. His first words to her didn't clear it up, either.

"You're not an Ice Queen." He stopped in front of her and held up the envelope, torn open unevenly. A good representation for how she'd felt over the last week. "This proves it."

She didn't follow his meaning, so she said some-thing neutral. "Paynes always repay their debts."

"You're not in debt to me. I'm in debt to you. You gave me the best gift of all." His mouth curved, re-minding her of the taste of his smile. "It didn't cost you a thing but it was far more valuable than anything you could've bought."

The dangerous emotions she'd packed down into

a tight ball at the bottom of her heart threatened to unravel. She crossed her arms tighter to keep it there.

"You showed me *you*. The real you. The unsure, vulnerable, shy you. And when it came time for me to man up and show you that part of me—" he shook his head "—I failed you."

That tight ball unraveled like a spring.

"This—" he held up the check inside the envelope "—is proof that you still love me."

She felt her cheeks go white as the blood drained from them to her toes. She shook her head. Not because it wasn't true but because he wasn't supposed to know that part. That check was intended to be proof that she *didn't* love him. She needed to learn how to be whole without him. She needed space and giving him the money he'd never wanted was supposed to guarantee that space. To allow her to close the door on what they had for good.

"You never would've sent me this if you didn't still love me. If you hated me, you wouldn't have given me another thought," he told her. "Like I said, you're not the Ice Queen. In fact, everything about you is fire. From your red hair to your flaming honesty to the way you heat me up with your vulnerability. I thought I'd walk away and save us both further pain but the truth is… I'm scorched, Andy. *Ruined.* I will never again be whole. Not without you."

She closed her eyes and sensed Gage stepping close to her. She'd never imagined this scenario—not in all her multiple-choice options. He'd given a speech that absolutely owned her in the threshold of her apartment.

And he wasn't through yet.

"I was trying to rebuild my own walls and failing miserably. I fell in love with you, and because I'm so hopelessly out of practice at responding to that much love, I blew it. I had a chance to claim your heart and defend your honor and I didn't."

"The pact…" were the only words she could utter. She couldn't address the "fell in love" part or the fact that she'd "scorched" him and "ruined" him for all others. That was too big.

"Fuck the pact."

She took him in—those boyish curls and caramel-brown eyes. The way being near him felt so, so right.

"If I promise to love you forever, will you forgive me?"

"I…" But more words wouldn't come.

"If I promise to be brave from now on out, can you let me in?"

A shaky nod was the most she could give him before she covered her mouth to stifle the cry. Then she was in Gage's arms, being held and shushed, the words *I'm sorry* and *I love you* on a loop on his tongue.

When he let her go, he held the envelope between them. "An Ice Queen would've kept the money as the ultimate screw-you. You, Andrea Payne, are no Ice Queen."

He tore the envelope in half and then in half again and dropped the pieces at their feet. His eyes flicked to her lips and just like before their first kiss, he said, "I'll let you come to me."

She gripped the back of his neck. "But you'll give as good as you get?"

"You bet your perfect breasts I will."

They met in the middle, their mouths crashing and their bodies fusing together—as close as they could get without being naked. But they were naked in another way—their souls had been bared.

Walls had come down.

Hearts could heal.

Pacts, like the envelope at her feet, could be torn into pieces.

"I missed you," she whispered, the tear sliding down her cheek a happy one.

He thumbed it away and smiled warmly. "You'll never have to miss me again."

Epilogue

It was a gorgeous, sunshiny, perfect day to be on the water.

The pontoon swayed gently in the cove where they'd anchored, Andy's four sisters holding out their flutes while Gage filled each to the brim with sparkling rosé.

It was a beautiful summer day in Crown, Ohio.

"Carrying forth the tradition of the couples' cruise was never not an option," Andy explained as she pulled out a plastic flute for herself. Gage winked as he uncorked a second bottle and filled Andy's glass as well as his own. "This time around, we have a new couple who will reenact a movie kiss and attempt to steal first place from Gage and me."

"A tough act to follow," Gwen offered. "Good luck, Ness."

All heads swiveled to Vanessa and her date, Mitch-ell. Mitch was forty years old, had two daughters who were ten and eight, though they hadn't come to the Payne-Fleming wedding, and he had a nice smile and a smooth-as-butter Southern accent.

Andy liked Mitch.

Vanessa and Alec had gone to counseling, and al-though it didn't result in a reunion, Ness was much happier with her new beau. Andy could see it in the loose way she draped over him on the boat's seat. Sometimes things had to break to be fixed, like Andy and Gage, but other times the break was too final and new parts were needed.

"We're a hard act to follow," Gage said. "Andy and I nailed *Titanic*."

A round of teasing "ohhs" lifted on the air.

"You say that like we didn't prepare." Ness arched one eyebrow in challenge.

"I know better." Andy playfully rolled her eyes. Vanessa and Alec had rehearsed for their *Dirty Dancing* kiss for weeks.

"Get ready to be dazzled. But not yet. We have to practice. Into the water with all of you." Ness shooed them off the boat.

"Not a hard sell today." Gage polished off his bub-bly and stripped his shirt over his head. The late July afternoon was a stifling ninety-eight degrees and the humidity was set to "stun."

Within minutes of Gage cannonballing off the side of the boat, everyone save Ness and Mitch was in the water.

Arm around her waist, Gage tugged Andy to him and she wrapped her legs around him.

"God, they're as bad as we were," Gwen told Garrett.

"Worse," her husband concluded.

"Do you think they're really going to beat our couples' cruise kiss?" Gage asked Andy, ignoring the ribbing of her family to nuzzle her nose.

She held onto her gorgeous fiancé, squinting against the blindingly bright sun. "Possibly. Ness hates to lose."

"Sounds like she has a lot to learn." His eyebrows jumped in self-deprecating humor. At one point he'd been the one who was so afraid to fail he hadn't given them a chance.

He'd come a long way. Especially when he proposed at Monarch Consulting. He'd lured her to the building under the guise of meeting for lunch and then was on his knees before her, proclaiming his love for her in front of his friends.

Andy pulled her hand out of the water to admire the engagement ring. A teardrop-shaped diamond with smaller stones on the band. Gage had told her he liked to think that it was shaped like a flame.

She liked that, too.

"We're ready! Although you're going to get the PG version." Ness came out from behind the beach towel Mitch had used to shield her and stood on one of the boat's seats. She was wearing a short pink skirt, an argyle-patterned neckerchief and knee socks in the same jaunty design. Her hair was pulled back at the sides but distinctly ruffled to make her look like she'd had a few too many.

Once the song started playing, Gwen gasped. "I know this one! I know it!"

Andy watched the scene unfold, from Ness leading Mitch across the boat to her falling on a seat and letting out a loud laugh. By the time she tossed aside the kerchief and they vanished from sight, Kelli and Gwen were cheering.

Carroll was grinning, too. The husbands, including Andy's husband-to-be, looked as clueless as she felt.

Vanessa popped back into view, Mitch with her. "Sorry the kiss happened out of sight. We got a little carried away. Any guesses?"

"*The Wedding Date*, and bravo," Kelli answered.

"Yes!" Vanessa shot her fists into the air as everyone clapped.

"What movie?" Andy had to ask.

Gwen looked affronted. "Debra Messing. Dermot Mulroney. The boat scene."

"The movie where she pays the guy to be her date for her sister's wedding. Total fiction, right?" Vanessa added with a wink.

Next to her Gage laughed. "That was a good one."

"The best!" Ness corrected, and then awarded herself first place.

"Close," Gage murmured as he pulled Andy into his arms. Then he whispered so that only she could hear, "But not the best."

* * * * *

Drew Fleming recognizes her older brother's sexiest best friend immediately, even if Reid doesn't recognize her. But after one fantasy night together, Reid discovers he just slept with his best friend's little sister! All bets are off...or are they?

Reid's story is coming soon!
Available July 2019!

"You live in a secluded paradise." Rain started, a light sprinkling that grew stronger in seconds until it lashed the car windows. The interior immediately fogged—probably from her accelerated breathing.

Jack smiled. "There are other houses." The wipers added a rhythmic thrum to the sound of the rainfall. "The mature trees make it seem more remote than it is." Rather than take the driveway to the front of the house, he pulled around back to a carport. "The garage is filled with tools, so Brodie helped me put up a shelter as a temporary place to park."

Ronnie was too busy removing her seat belt and looking at the incredible surroundings to pay much attention to where he parked—until he turned off the engine. Then the intoxicating feel of his attention enveloped her.

Her gaze shot to his. *Think of your future*, she told herself. *Think of how he'll screw up the job if he sticks around.*

He'd half turned to face her, one forearm draped over the wheel. After his gaze traced every feature of her face with almost tactile concentration, he murmured, "We'll wait here just a minute to see if the storm blows over."

Here, in this small space? With only a console, their warm breath and hunger between them?

Did the man think she was made of stone?

She swallowed heavily, already tempted beyond measure. A boom of thunder resonated in her chest, and she barely noticed, not with her gaze locked on his and the tension ramping up with every heartbeat.

Suddenly she knew. No matter what happened with the job, regardless of how he might irk her, she'd never again experience sexual chemistry this strong and she'd be a fool not to explore it.

She'd like to think she wasn't a fool.

"Jack…" The word emerged as a barely there whisper, a question, an admission. Yearning.

As if he understood, he shifted toward her, his eyes gone darker with intent. "One kiss, Ronnie. I need that."

God, she needed it more. Anticipation sizzling, heart swelling, she met him halfway over the console.

His mouth grazed her cheek so very softly, leaving a trail of heat along her jaw, her chin. "You have incredible skin."

Skin? Who cared about her skin? "Kiss me."

"Yes, ma'am." As his lips finally met hers in a bold, firm press, his hand, so incredibly large, cupped the base of her skull and angled her for a perfect fit.

Ronnie was instantly lost.

She didn't recall reaching for him, but suddenly her fingers were buried in his hair and she somehow hung over the center console.

They were no longer poised between the seats, two mouths meeting in neutral ground. She pressed him back in his seat as she took the kiss she wanted, the kiss she needed.

Whether she opened her mouth to invite his tongue, or his tongue forged the way, she didn't know and honestly didn't care, not with the heady taste of him making her want more, more, *more*.

Don't miss Lori Foster's Slow Ride, *available soon from HQN Books!*

*Matt Richmond is the perfect man for Nadia Gonzalez,
except for one hitch—he's her boss! But when their
passion is too strong to resist, it isn't long before a
mysterious someone threatens to destroy everything
she's worked for…*

Read on for a sneak peek at
Tempted by Scandal *by Karen Booth!*

Nadia Gonzalez didn't believe in regrets. She simply did
her damnedest to never make a mistake. Being careful
but determined always paid off.

But there was a very good chance that Nadia had made
a mistake that put her job in jeopardy. She'd done the
unthinkable. She'd fallen into bed with her ridiculously
hot boss. A gaffe for the ages.

But the minute she saw Matt in a perfectly tailored
sleek black tux at the hospital fund-raiser last night,
looking unfairly handsome, she knew she was in trouble.
He almost never put on a tie. But as difficult as it was to
get Matt into a suit, it turned out that Nadia had a talent
for getting him out of it.

This was no small development in Nadia's life. She'd
spent the past fourteen months, virtually every moment
she'd been employed by Matt, secretly pining for him.
He was everything Nadia could ever want in a man, the
embodiment of sexy confidence, high IQ and seemingly

endless brilliance wrapped up in six feet two inches of the most appealing package Nadia could imagine, topped off with thick sandy-blond hair. When he walked into a room, men and women alike turned their heads. The air crackled with electricity. His mere arrival trumpeted his greatness, and was punctuated by his bracing blue eyes. Just thinking about him made her fingers and lips tingle.

Now, driving up a steep and winding hillside to The Opulence, an hour east of Seattle, her foot gunning the gas, these thoughts of Matt were ill-timed at best.

Yes, she'd wanted Matt for a long time and they'd shared an unbelievable night of passion. But so what? Was she really willing to throw away her career? No.

Was she willing to discount the years she'd scraped by so she could make a better life for herself and her family? Absolutely not.

Matt was not the settling-down type. There would be no happy ending with him. Which meant her first priority when speaking to him today would be to make sure he understood that last night was a onetime thing. They would both be better off if they forgot about it and returned to their strictly professional dynamic.

Even though that was going to break her heart.

Will they or won't they?

Don't miss what happens next!
Tempted by Scandal *by Karen Booth*

Available May 2019 wherever
Harlequin® Desire books and ebooks are sold.

www.Harlequin.com

HDEXP0419

Want to give in to temptation with
steamy tales of irresistible desire?

Check out **Harlequin® Presents®,
Harlequin® Desire** and
Harlequin® Kimani™ Romance books!

New books available every month!

CONNECT WITH US AT:

Facebook.com/groups/HarlequinConnection

Facebook.com/HarlequinBooks

Twitter.com/HarlequinBooks

Instagram.com/HarlequinBooks

Pinterest.com/HarlequinBooks

ReaderService.com

31192021658123